H L

TRAIL OF THE BURNED MAN

When Rafe Morgan rides into Twisted Oak, Wyoming, he gets into a saloon brawl and horribly disfigures an outlaw named Dutch Williams. Vowing revenge, Dutch and his men take two hostages, including the marshal's daughter. Rafe joins Deputy U.S. Marshal Ethan O'Hara's posse hunting for Dutch. But with the hostages as bait, Dutch wants blood, and he wants the posse destroyed. Following the outlaw's trail, the posse find themselves in a desperate struggle for their very lives.

THOMAS McNULTY

◆

TRAIL OF THE BURNED MAN

Complete and Unabridged

LINFORD
Leicester

First published in Great Britain in 2009 by
Robert Hale Limited
London

First Linford Edition
published 2010
by arrangement with
Robert Hale Limited
London

British Library CIP Data

McNulty, Thomas, *1955 –*
    Trail of the burned man. - -
    (Linford western library)
    1. Western stories.
    2. Large type books.
    I. Title II. Series
    813.6–dc22

    ISBN 978–1–44480–474–4

Published by
F. A. Thorpe (Publishing)
Anstey, Leicestershire

Set by Words & Graphics Ltd.
Anstey, Leicestershire
Printed and bound in Great Britain by
T. J. International Ltd., Padstow, Cornwall

*Dedicated to my wife Jan
and daughter Brenna,
With love*

1

The Fight

Spring 1876

Many years later the dime novelists would say that he killed thirty men and rode north to avoid being lynched, but this was all exaggeration. The truth is he was a simple man with his own brand of moral conviction. He learned the difference between right and wrong at a young age. The rest he learned in the way that all young men reared in Texas learn to avoid being trampled by an angry bull.

He rode into the Wyoming territory with the intent of hiring on as a ranch hand for one of the cattle outfits. He had no way of knowing the tribulations he would endure. He came up through the plains and crossed into the Wyoming territory seven weeks after leaving Texas. In his pocket he carried a letter of introduction from his former employer.

He had come to a town called Twisted Oak not far from the Wind River. He crested a hill and looked down at the settlement. Woodsmoke drifted from a few chimneys. The town sat low in a valley near the river and in the shadow of mountains. Rafael Morgan urged his horse along the sloping trail. By the time he reached the outskirts of the town the sun had gone down. He rode into the town in darkness.

Twisted Oak was sprawled along the western edge of the valley. There were small ranch houses along the perimeter and the main street was crowded with businesses — a feed store and hardware supply companies, an assay office, a bank, a clothing store, a sheriff's office, a hotel, several restaurants and saloons, a blacksmith and livery, and even a newspaper office. Down at the end of the main street there was a new church with a freshly painted steeple. The Cattlemen's Association had some stockyards on the eastern end. The place had a permanent feel to it.

Rafe Morgan was tall, sandy-haired, slender but well muscled. His blue eyes appraised everything around him without judgment but wary for trouble. He had seen much in his twenty-six years and was accustomed to life on the trail or as a cowhand. He could survive on his own along a trail, killing whatever game he needed for food. But he preferred the life of a cowhand because it offered a sense of satisfaction in a day's hard work. He knew there was more to life than cowpunching, and he had a taste for knowledge, too.

As he approached a cluster of buildings he instinctively dropped his right hand to the walnut grip of the Colt resting in his buscadero style holster. He didn't think it was likely he would find trouble here, but old habits are hard to break. The Colt, along with the 1866 Henry rifle in his leather scabbard, had saved him from trouble often enough. The Henry had belonged to his father and just a year before he had had a gunsmith replace the trigger spring and file the bolt so that the lever snapped open as if it were greased with butter.

He reined his horse down a side street where he found a boy named Bobby at the livery who agreed to keep his saddle-bags and the Henry in the livery office and away from curious eyes. He didn't own much, but he would keep what he owned. His belongings amounted to his weapons, ammunition, two wool shirts folded neatly in the saddle-bags, an extra pair of trousers, a comb made of buffalo bone, a mackinaw coat, a tin cup and plate, a small coffee pot, a box of matches, a Bowie knife and his mother's Bible.

The boy seemed earnest and he asked him to rub his horse down and give him plenty of oats. Rafe unsaddled the horse himself and led the animal into a stall.

'Where you from?' the boy asked.

'Texas. Been riding about six weeks. Where can I get a drink?'

Rafe didn't want to be rude, but he also didn't want to offer too much information about himself, so he answered questions bluntly but with enough content to satisfy most strangers.

'The Valediction Saloon is the place tonight. Some cowpunchers rode in earlier and they've been drinking ever since.'

'What did you say your name was?'

'Bobby Shepard.'

'Well, Bobby Shepard, here's a few extra dollars to make sure that Henry rifle doesn't get lost. It belonged to my pa.'

Rafe found the saloon a few minutes later. He pushed through the batwing doors and quickly assessed the crowd. A half-dozen men, all wearing guns, were lined up at the bar, each with a dusty boot propped on the brass rail. Another dozen were dispersed at tables playing cards or at the faro table. A few soiled doves, young and lovely but already looking tired and bored, served drinks or stood about pretending to be interested in the card games. A few of them had already seen him walk in and were assessing him as a potential customer.

He edged himself into the noisy group and waited for the barman. He only wanted a few drinks to settle himself down after the long ride. Afterward he would find the hotel and bunk down for the night.

'What's your pleasure?' The barman asked without looking at him. He was a small but solid-looking man. His eyes were flicking nervously toward a noisy group playing poker near the pot-bellied stove.

'Just a beer.'

Rafe sipped the foamy beer. The cold beer swept into his belly while he examined the painting on the wall

6

behind the bar. A plump, nude woman swathed in pink silk smiled at him from a velvet couch.

Rafe was working on his second beer and feeling content that his long ride had gone so well. Not that many weeks ago he had crossed the Red River, following the worn cattle trails to Fort Leavenworth before turning west and picking up a trail that ran parallel to the Platte River. He followed the Platte River northeast until he crossed the Sweetwater Rim. He had taken a slow, circuitous route, sometimes lingering in small towns for a day or two. Several times he had good campsites and stayed several days fishing along creeks or small rivers. There had been no hurry to present his letter of reference. All he had wanted was to put his past behind him.

He knew that anyone observing him now would appraise the small flat-brimmed hat, the Bowie knife in its sheath and the .45 Colt in his holster and view him as a common Westerner.

He gave no outward appearance of hostility. He was what he seemed; a saddle-tramp, a hired hand between jobs.

He heard voices raised in anger and glanced back at the card players.

'Too many damn Indians still in the territory!' one man said.

'And too many barkeeps serving cheap whiskey!' another added.

The two men moved up to the bar and demanded more whiskey.

Rafe heard the barman say 'That's the best we have,' as the two men set their glasses on the bar. A space had widened in the crowd. Men shuffled away, careful not to look at the two drunk cowhands.

'Then fill these glasses quick if that's the best you have!'

The barmen eyed them warily as they drank. They made a few more rude comments before returning to their card game.

The tension in the room was palpable and Rafe was thinking about that letter of reference in his pocket. In the morning he would present his letter to the marshal the way he planned. If he was lucky he'd find a job on one of the outlying ranches.

The beer had made him realize how tired he was. Rafe glanced at the drunks. One of them was tall with hair the color of pewter and small dark eyes. His thin lips were chomped onto a thin cigar. The other man was a Mexican; fat and short, but one look at the Mexican's face and Rafe knew he was dangerous.

'What the hell you lookin' at?'

The man with the pewter hair was glaring at Rafe. In his peripheral vision Rafe noticed the bartender stop, turn and look his way.

Rafe knew the bartender had a shotgun down behind the bar, but he wouldn't go for it. He didn't figure he was the type to use a gun. He wouldn't want anything to do with that. It would get him killed, Rafe thought, so he'll avoid the shotgun.

Rafe looked away, sipped his beer.

'Goddamn, you deaf?'

Rafe watched the two men in the bar's mirror. The Mexican stepped back, giving the taller man room. They were watching him as if he were a diseased dog that needed killing. Rafe looked at the tall man, held his gaze.

'No offense meant. I'm just shaking the trail dust from my throat.'

'Where you from?' It was a command, not a question and Rafe felt his pulse quicken.

'I don't rightly see how that's your business.'

The man was raging drunk. Rafe glanced back at the poker tables. Most everyone in the saloon was watching. They were all drunk, too. Rafe saw it in their faces, a pure discontentment and fury. A sadness swept over him as he accepted that he'd walked right into a damned hornet's nest.

'You a sheepherder? Ask the boys here what happened to the last sheepherder that came into this territory.'

Rafe regarded the man solemnly. There was nothing worse than an insolent drunk looking for a fight and Rafe had had his fill of that down in Texas. The Mexican eyed him warily. The tall drunk continued staring at Rafe.

The bartender came up and set two fresh whiskeys on the bar.

'Dutch, these are on the house. We don't need any trouble.'

Their attention diverted, the man called Dutch and his Mexican friend sipped their whiskey. Dutch wore a gun and a long leather coat. His spurs clanged like music as he reeled back and spat in the barman's face.

'Your whiskey's no good!'

Rafe felt pressure in his temples and the muscles in his legs twist into knots. The barman's face reddened as he wiped the spittle with his sleeve, but as Rafe expected he didn't go for the shotgun.

'It's the best we have,' the bartender said.

Rafe noticed he was trembling. He felt sympathy for the man. He was in no position to retaliate against a drunken cowpuncher who would be quick to draw. Rafe looked around. No one looked much interested in the bartender's problem; the girls loitering around the card tables looked a little interested, like maybe a good fight would liven up their dull evening. None of the card players looked like they would lend a hand if trouble started. They drank in silence and for a moment Rafe thought the potential for trouble had passed.

'Give me the bottle!' Dutch barked. 'This had better be good whiskey or I'll put a hole in you.'

Dutch spat his whiskey across the bar, cursed, and shifted the bottle to his left hand. Rafe saw the movement, the man's shoulder dropping as he went for his gun. He stepped behind him as the gun came up and Rafe kicked him between the legs from behind. He heard the breath leave the man's lungs as he doubled over. Rafe snatched away the

12

gun and tossed it to the barman. He grabbed the bottle and poured the contents over Dutch's head.

'You need to cool down, pardner.'

The place was quiet now as Dutch crouched in pain on the floor. Before anyone else could move Rafe stepped up close to the Mexican, yanked his gun from its holster and held it up under his chin. The Mexican's black eyes went wide.

'Go have a seat and you'll get your gun back later.'

The Mexican stepped back, rage reddening his face, but he reluctantly eased himself onto a chair.

Rafe stepped up to the brass rail, watching the poker tables in the big mirror behind the bar. He set the Mexican's Colt on the bar next to Dutch's. So far so good, he thought. He'd disarmed the two trouble-makers. Now he could finish his drink and be on his way. He felt the unfriendly eyes of the card hustlers and cattlemen watching him as he pulled a small pouch of tobacco from his vest pocket and began rolling a smoke. Dutch was still bent over, his breath coming in heaving gulps. He said something that might have been a curse.

'I'll . . . teach you . . . a thing . . . or two . . . ' Dutch rasped out the words.

Rafe had to restrain himself from laughing out loud. Drunks always had a way of talking big. The fools never knew when enough was enough.

But the tension in the room was palpable. Rafe's every sense was alert as he pretended nonchalance. He leaned back against the bar while he rolled the cigarette and summed up the crowd at the table. There were four of them, and they represented his strongest threat now. They wouldn't take kindly to their friend being kicked. They watched him with the cold, flat eyes of hard men who never knew kindness. The other two were no better. Hard, surly cattlemen or drifters.

Rafe had the cigarette rolled and picked up the sputtering oil lamp from the scarred bartop. He was about to lift off the glass funnel and light his smoke when Dutch sprang from the floor and lunged forward, fists balled. Rafe had enough time to spin and slam the oil lamp on to Dutch's head. The lamp splintered and sparks jumped into Dutch's sopping hair. The alcohol and kerosene in his hair ignited. His head was engulfed in flames.

Rafe had instinctively drawn his gun and held it level. Dutch swiveled on his feet, reminding Rafe of a dog chasing its tail. When he circled near, Rafe kicked him a second time between the legs. Dutch went down with a loud grunt. For a moment there was no sound from the stunned audience. They watched in astonishment as Dutch thrashed on the floor, trying to twist away from his burning flesh.

Then there was the sound of chairs pushing back, creaking leather, and spurs jingling. Rafe turned his gun on the angry group. They stopped. The sound of the Dutch's sizzling head was ominously loud. Dutch began wailing; short, plaintive cries.

Someone in the crowd said, 'You might wanna put that fire out!' Then the barman came around with a bucket of water and emptied it over Dutch's head. Wisps of smoke rose up and filled the room with the stench of burned flesh.

The Mexican looked at Rafe with disgust. Someone said, 'Goddamn you! You burned the hell out of him!'

Dutch was groaning at Rafe's feet, holding his charred head with both hands. Rafe appraised the men he held at bay. He had little chance with them, he knew. Only the fact he held a gun on them at close quarters kept him alive. But it wouldn't last. He recognized the hatred and determination in their eyes. Somebody would try him. At least one of them would take the chance, drawing and firing, and then all hell would break loose. Once a gun was fired everybody would be shooting. He had seconds to make up his mind.

Rafe was moving as he made the choice, backstepping to the batwing doors, his gun swinging back and forth across the line of men. To hell with this. It was time to leave.

The burned man, still crouched and groaning, lifted his head. 'Damn your eyes!' he hissed, 'I'll see you again, and when I do I'll destroy this town and you along with it!'

A chill went down Rafe's spine as he turned and stepped on to the board-walk.

The stables were at the far end of the street. They would be on him before he could traverse that distance. He looked around, hoping to find an open alley, but at the same instant realized his plight might be hopeless. He didn't know the layout of the town. There were hoarse yells as he rushed along the boardwalk, pushing himself with long strides away from the saloon. Another second and he expected to hear gunfire. He waited a few seconds and watched. Nothing moved. Cursing again under his breath, he turned down an alley, swerving through the darkness. He turned again, ducking behind a building, trying to make his way back toward his horse. He would have to go around the building and come at the livery from the other side.

He encountered a waist-high adobe wall and he jumped on it, dropped to the other side and ran to the end. At the far end he leapt over the wall into another alley.

He knew some of those men would be after him, but the others would probably leave him alone. He had only offended one group, but there was always the possibility that someone itching for a fight would join the search. But a few of them would follow for certain. He moved along the wall and looked into the street. He was surprised the street was empty. The stables were thirty feet away.

He heard the sharp clang of a spur a second before two men were on him. A fist smashed his lips and he reeled back.

He hadn't wanted any trouble, but here it was hitting him in the face. He had come into town wanting only a drink and a place to rest before presenting his letter of reference.

He hit the ground hard and rolled, coming up in a swirl of dust. He backed up, letting them come close, then he held his ground and waited. It was dark and perhaps they thought he was finished. Another fist was aimed at his head and he ducked and hit the man hard in the chest. He set himself and shot another fist into the man's face. The man went down, grunting.

He was already sweating as he waded into the other man, swinging hard. There was a singular pleasure for him as his knuckles split a nose open, then a mouth. His second opponent was down, holding his face and spitting blood.

So far no one had fired a gun. They were being careful. The thought flashed through Rafe's mind that it was because a Deputy US Marshal made his home here. They didn't want to draw attention to themselves. That might give him some time. Get to his horse. Ride on to Jackson Hole.

He was down before he knew it, his head throbbing under the impact of a gun-butt. He tried to roll away but he was kicked solidly in the stomach. They dragged him to his feet and one man held his arms behind him while the other began hitting him, quick iron punches to the ribs. In the dim moonlight he recognized one of the men as the stocky Mexican.

There was no thinking about it now, no time for contemplation. He spun wildly and the man holding him took the next punch. He broke free, lashing out. The anger and blood-lust had taken over as he pounded the man. The two men were battering each other with bloody fists. Rafe threw hard punches, aiming for the man's head. He snapped his balled fist into the man's eyes, at his mouth, at his nose. One last hard punch slammed him to the ground.

'All I wanted was a drink,' he said, taking a lung-full of air, 'and you men should have left me alone.'

To his astonishment the two men jumped to their feet and bolted, vanishing down the dark alley. The sudden end of the attack momentarily took him by surprise. To hell with them, Rafe thought. He took a breath and composed himself, his eyes flicking back and forth as he waited for the men to rush him again. But the street was empty.

With a shrug he went to the stables. There was no sign of the kid so Rafe found his horse and was unraveling the bridle when he heard footsteps behind him. He turned quickly, expecting another fight, but stopped at the sight of the man before him. He was a tall, mustached man wearing a tin star and holding his gun level with Rafe's belly.

'You gave those men a good fight,' the marshal said. 'But that's about as far as you go.'

2

Dilemma

10 March 1876

Dear Ethan

The bearer of this letter is Rafael Morgan for whom I am serving as reference and will stand the test of inquiry for those doubting his strength of character. It is true that Mr. Morgan has earned a reputation for possessing a quarrelsome disposition but I hasten to add this reputation is unjustified and solely the product of wagging tongues.

Ethan, I do not propose to be a burden, but I am if not wise then passionate in my judgment of this young man who reminds me slightly of myself and certainly a great deal of you. Perhaps I am doddering in my old age, but this young man deserves a better chance than he will get here.

I believe he has sufficient funds which he earned and saved, a remarkable trait in itself; and if he can find satisfactory employment for several years he might yet stake himself to a reasonable parcel of land and become something more than a hired gun.

Sincerely yours,
R.J. Hogan

Deputy US Marshal Ethan O'Hara folded the letter and returned it to his vest pocket. He sipped his coffee and mulled over the events of the previous evening. He was sitting alone at a table in Bradbury's Restaurant and finishing up a breakfast of steak and eggs, taking time to put his thoughts together.

He was a dark-haired man with a handlebar mustache and piercing green eyes. He wore brown trousers and a dark-blue shirt and a leather vest his wife had made twenty years before. In his vest pocket he carried his father's gold watch. Often, he would palm the watch, snap open the worn casing, and stare at the small daguerreotypes of his mother and wife while pretending to check the time. Ethan O'Hara was not a man given to public sentiment and he preferred the pretense of a punctual man.

There was no reason to hold the man he arrested last night. The bartender, Dan Haycroft, made it clear what happened. Dan interrupted Ethan at Doc Parker's weekly poker game and told him there was a fight at the Valediction. Irritated from being interrupted during a winning streak, Ethan grudgingly went out to see what all the uproar was about. He found Rafe fighting in the stables and decided to hold him overnight. Alerted to Ethan's presence, Rafe's attackers had disappeared quickly and the marshal wasn't in the mood to go chasing drunks in the dark. He settled on locking up Rafe and sorting out the rest come morning.

Then there was the matter of Dutch Williams. Dan Haycroft had said that Dutch was seriously burned, but the cattleman had refused treatment by Doc Parker. Ethan didn't care much for Dutch, and he liked his reputation even less. Dutch was trouble.

Last night, with Rafe Morgan locked up in a cell, Ethan chose the office bunk over his usual bed at the hotel; a habit he had acquired long ago of sleeping in the jail when any of the three cells was occupied.

The letter from R.J. shed light on Rafe Morgan's past, and he didn't care much for that either. The morning was shaping up with too many elements that Ethan didn't care for.

It was the letter's signature that made the difference. Ethan smiled to himself remembering those years long ago when he rode with R.J. as a pony express rider and hunted buffalo in the Dakotas. Ethan hadn't seen the man in twenty-five years but he trusted him implicitly. Still, it troubled him that Rafe had come into trouble so quickly. Some folks had a knack for trouble and this young man had run right into it when he met Dutch Williams.

Ethan sighed and finished his coffee. He wanted to talk to Dan Haycroft again before letting Rafe Morgan out of jail. Another hour in the cell wouldn't hurt that young man at all.

He found Dan at the Valediction Saloon, sweeping the place clean.

'Good morning, Ethan.'

'Good morning, Dan. I want you to tell me again what happened last night.'

'Like I said yesterday, Ethan, it was Dutch Williams and his boys,' Dan said. 'They were here drinking and playing cards. It was getting rough. They were giving me some grief.'

'And this drifter didn't do anything to provoke them?'

'Not a thing, no sir. He probably saved my hide. Those men are the most trouble we've seen around here in a long time. Nothing good will come of any of this.'

'We agree on that.'

'Who is that fella anyhow?'

'His name's Rafe Morgan, from Texas.'

'Well, I'm indebted to him.' Dan cast an embarrassed downward glance as he swept a cloth over the bar. 'Dutch spit in my face and was pulling the hammer back when this fellow stopped him.'

Ethan was surprised. Being humiliated like that set his blood boiling. Rafe Morgan had done exactly what Ethan would have done in the same situation.

Ethan had questioned a few of the girls Dan had working for him and they all told the same story. It was clear Rafe had interceded on behalf of the barman.

'I guess it was lucky this cowboy happened along when he did.'

'That's a fact, Ethan, although I wouldn't say he's happy about it now.'

'No, he isn't. Being in jail takes the jingle out of a man's spurs right quick.'

Everything seemed clear cut except the letter was a surprise. The way Rafe Morgan handed over the letter, calm and naturally just after Ethan locked him in a cell, slipping the folded letter between the bars as he said, 'This here letter of reference is from Mr R.J. Hogan down in Texas.' The way he said it, matter of factly, took him by surprise. It was not every cowpuncher who got himself locked up that had a letter of reference from Mr R.J. Hogan down in Texas.

What Ethan hadn't told anyone were the stories he'd heard about Rafe; little tales that drifted out from the round-ups and saloons. The young cowhand had a reputation for being fast with a gun. Ethan had heard that Rafe stood his ground against a cattle baron named Quincey when he rode for his old friend R.J. Hogan down near the Red River. Hogan also carried a reputation — that of a fair and sturdy Westerner who knew his way around.

He couldn't put it off any longer. He had to let the cowpuncher go. Ethan made his way back to the jail, his boots kicking up dust on the street. It was going to be another hot day and he just hoped the appearance of Rafe Morgan wouldn't make things hotter in the territory than they already were.

He found Bobby Shepard sitting in his chair with his feet on the desk and reading a magazine about Davy Crockett. His nose was in the magazine and his cowlick stuck up above the pages. Ethan slammed the door and Bobby jumped to his feet.

'You need a haircut, Bobby.'

'Aw, Ethan . . . '

Bobby was an orphan and lived in a small room in back of the Valediction Saloon. He did chores for Dan Haycroft to earn his keep, and helped out at the stables, but the boy spent a lot of time hanging around the jail asking Ethan about the war. Bobby had a curiosity that wouldn't quit.

'I heard what happened. He came to

the stable last night and I fed his horse for him.'

Ethan ignored him and went to the cell. Rafe was on the cot, apparently sleeping, but Ethan knew better. A man like Rafe Morgan wouldn't be sleeping at all.

'Bobby, unlock this cell.'

Rafe had been motionless on the cot, hat tipped over his eyes, but now he swung his legs around and pushed his hat back. Bobby unlocked the cell and Rafe came out holding his hat. 'Thanks, Marshal. I'm sorry for all this trouble.'

'The trouble rode into town before you did,' Ethan said. 'You'll be glad to be on your way.'

'I was expecting to stay awhile.'

'I figured as much when I read that letter. You won't like it then when I say I'd prefer that you rode on.'

Ethan went to his desk, opened the drawer and pulled out Rafe's gun and holster. He gave the bundle to Rafe and waited while he buckled the holster to his hips.

'Your horse is still at the livery. Adam Washington runs the livery and blacksmith shop. You can settle up with him.'

Rafe appraised the stoic lawman. 'Does that letter hold any weight with you?'

Ethan shrugged.

'It tells me R.J. trusts you and I suppose that counts for something.'

'I'm looking for a job.'

'You'll be lucky to find that around here.'

'That doesn't sound encouraging. Mr Hogan thought you might lend a hand.'

'I'm not in the encouragement business.'

Ethan sat down at his desk and began a process of pretending to examine some papers, but Rafe wasn't ready to end the conversation yet.

'Any idea what happened to the man I fought?'

Ethan stopped ruffling the papers and looked at Rafe.

'You're talking about someone that is more trouble than I care to see in this

31

territory. His name is Dutch Williams. He rode out with four men. One of them is a Mexican named Carlos Duranos. Dutch had a ranch east of here a few years ago but lost his cattle to hoof and mouth. Word is he wasn't much of a rancher to begin with. What I've heard about him I won't repeat in the presence of decent people.'

'What exactly makes him trouble-some?'

'Just rumors or he'd be in jail. Some men have a shine to 'em that isn't clean.'

Ethan wasn't telling Rafe that Dutch and his men were suspects in a series of bank robberies across the territory. Several witnesses had come forward and stated that even though the bandits wore bandannas over their faces they'd recognized his voice. It wasn't enough to put him in jail, but it was enough for Ethan to wonder why Dutch and his men had come to town. He was convinced they were sizing up the bank, and if that was true, then Rafe's unexpected encounter with Dutch added another facet of trouble to a dangerous situation. Ethan didn't like it at all.

'Marshal, he didn't seem that tough of a man,' Rafe said.

Ethan leaned back in his chair. 'It's not about being tough, not in the way you're thinking. If you stay in town I'll expect no trouble from you, and stay away from Dutch and his men.'

'I wasn't planning on looking for trouble.'

'We both know how trouble happens. I've seen your type before and I'm looking forward to your departure.'

'Don't stretch yourself making me feel welcome.'

Ethan watched him from under the brim of his hat. Rafe thought it over for a moment and then said, 'I'd be obliged if you gave some thought about a job around here. If you think of something I'll be at the hotel.'

'I hope it works out for you.' Ethan paused. 'R.J.'s letter says you have some money. I wouldn't go flashing it around.'

'I'm not stupid, Marshal.'

'Even an intelligent man makes mistakes. You might be paying a bill and somebody sees how much you have. Then there's trouble.'

'So I'll be careful and you don't have to worry about it.'

'They pay me to worry about it.'

Rafe gave a shrug, not liking the way things were going. Signaling an end to their conversation, Ethan turned abruptly to Bobby and said: 'Bobby, help Mr Morgan get situated at the hotel if that's still what he has a mind to do.'

They went out but Bobby stopped at he door and looked back at Ethan. 'You heard that Dutch vowed to destroy the town?'

'I heard.'

'You want me to ride out and see if I can find their camp?'

Ethan frowned. Bobby's cowlick was as thick as his enthusiasm. 'Not this time, Bobby.'

The disappointment was evident in

Bobby's face, but he didn't protest. The boy gave a reluctant nod and went out.

Ethan watched them from his window. That Rafe Morgan had brass. Ethan chuckled to himself thinking about Rafe's comment — 'Don't stretch yourself making me feel welcome.' That was rich, all right. He hadn't hesitated to come back at him with that remark. R.J. had been right, Rafe was a lot like him when he was younger. If Dutch hadn't been injured he might have been a tad more accommodating to the young man, but he couldn't take that chance now. The best thing for Rafe Morgan at this point was to keep riding.

Ten years of being the law in northern Wyoming had been a time-consuming responsibility; and now there were more cattle drives passing through the valley, and with the cattle came the men — drifters and gunfighters and men looking for a place to settle. It was getting to be a little too noisy in the territory, and he found the prospect of a long, hot summer unsettling.

He looked out at the dusty street simmering in the noonday sun.

R.J.'s letter hadn't made any effort in disguising the fact he expected Ethan to help Rafe find employment. That was just fine, Ethan thought, and now I'm stuck playing nursemaid to a cowboy with a reputation. The thought rankled him.

There were too many strangers in town lately, and more than a few appeared to be acquaintances of Dutch Williams. He wasn't going to have time to help Rafe secure employment even if he wanted to. The young man would have to fend for himself, and that's what worried Ethan the most.

★   ★   ★

The following morning Rafe heard birdsong filter up from the cottonwoods behind the hotel as he rubbed the sleep from his eyes. He heard the rattle of a buckboard as it went past and vague voices in the hall. All the familiar sounds of a town awakening.

He washed his face and dressed, settling his gun belt around his hips. An old familiar weight that seemed a part of him.

The long sleep had been good for him. He was exhausted when he arrived at the hotel and went to bed early without eating. He slept heavily but he dreamed of the man with the burned face. A shadowed figure awaited him behind the veil and when he went for his gun his holster was empty. It was like sinking in a foggy marsh or easing into the quicksand, and when the dark figure loomed closer he saw the scarred visage of Dutch Williams. When he awoke the dream moved away slowly like a snake slipping into a thicket before a storm.

Rafe pulled on his clothes and went out. He could smell the freshness of the earth as the sun burned away the dew. An early, warm spring was good for the ranchers and cattlemen. The grass would grow quickly and there would be great activity between Jackson Hole and Helena.

He had taken only a few steps when he saw something that made his pulse quicken: a young woman carrying several packages was coming out of the hardware store. Rafe admired her firm figure as she began loading the packages into a buckboard.

She had thick curly red hair that cascaded to her shoulders. A few strands of hair fell across her forehead catching the sun when she looked across at him and smiled. She was a breathtaking beauty with a softly curved body. She wore a simple gingham dress and leather riding boots. Her figure was compact but ample. Rafe crossed the street in long strides.

'Let me help you,' he said, taking a parcel from her hand and placing it in the buckboard, 'I'm Rafe Morgan.'

She looked at him, her blue eyes bright with interest. 'You were the talk of the town at breakfast this morning. Don't you belong in jail?' Her gaze held his and her mouth crinkled into a tiny smile. Just like that, easing into it like old friends.

'That was just a misunderstanding between the marshal and me,' Rafe said quickly, 'I had a little trouble at the saloon.'

'Is that so,' she mused, 'what kind of trouble was that?'

'Nothing important really. Some men were causing the barman some trouble and I ended up in the middle of a fracas.' Rafe looked around and said, 'This is a nice little town. I'm hoping to find work but the marshal said the prospects around here were slim.'

'I wouldn't know.' She eyed him intently. 'I'm afraid you've caught me at a busy time and I really must be going. It's been a pleasure meeting you, Mr Morgan.'

And with the same ease cut it off before they got too friendly, Rafe thought.

'I hope to see you around, ma'am,' he said.

Without answering she climbed up on the buckboard and gripped the reins. She looked him over one more time.

'Stay out of trouble, cowboy.' She snapped the leather and was off.

Rafe watched her go and a full minute passed before he realized he hadn't asked her name. He went to the livery to check on his horse. The blacksmith and livery owner was a tall, muscular black man who paused at the anvil and watched Rafe as he approached. Rafe was quickly becoming accustomed to being stared at. People had been looking him over since he rode into town, and he didn't figure they would stop until their curiosity was satisfied.

'I'm looking for Adam Washington.'

'You found him.'

'I thought I'd check on my horse.'

'You can see for yourself she's doing fine.'

The man nodded at the stable behind the blacksmith shop. 'I pulled a stone from her shoe and tightened a loose shoe on her back left leg.'

Rafe walked through the barn and entered the stable where he found his horse. The stable was clean and there was hay and water. Satisfied the animal was well cared for, Rafe went back and watched the blacksmith pounding out a gleaming new horseshoe with a hammer. The man's forearm bulged as he swept the hammer down on to the steaming metal. The sound of his efforts rang like a bell in the tiny barn.

'I'd like to pay what I owe so far. I might be around a couple of more days, and I can pay you for that as well.'

The man paused again, ribbons of sweat gleaming on his face.

'You don't have to pay me now. I'd rather take it all at once when you're ready to go.'

'Fair enough. I'm Rafe Morgan.'

'I know who you are. Ethan came by

already and said I could be expecting you.'

'I think the marshal gets a lot of respect around here.'

'He's earned it.'

Rafe wanted to talk some more but the blacksmith seemed reticent. They looked at each other a moment without speaking before the blacksmith turned back to the anvil.

Rafe said 'Well, thanks.' But the clang of the hammer drowned out the sound of his voice. Either that, or the blacksmith had no further interest in him.

Rafe reminded himself he wanted to stick around and find work. And there was another issue that he had to settle as well. He thought of it as his hand unconsciously dropped to his belt, his finger tracing the line of the money-belt he wore concealed under his clothes. A thousand hard-earned dollars that could be a start for him somewhere if he was careful. R.J. advised he deposit the money in a bank when he reached town but he didn't trust banks; yet he recognized the risk he was taking by carrying such a large sum in cash. Another day or two wouldn't hurt, he thought, and it might offer him some time to track down some employment prospects before turning his money over to a banker. But Ethan's remark that he would be lucky to find work nagged him.

A decade earlier he had taken a job on a cattle drive in San Antonio after his father died. He had only a little schooling, but he could read. At twenty-five he had no prospects except as a saddle-tramp or cowpuncher. Ten years of camps and long trails. Some of the memories were good. When it was new to him he enjoyed the warm nights under the endless stars and the low, nostalgic talk of the men around the campfire. He learned to love the land. More importantly, he learned to survive the hard, cold winters. But lately he decided he wanted to end his days on the long trail. He wanted to settle down, to find a place to belong to.

His natural ability, honed in his youth during the long drives when the boys were restless and made bets on knocking a tin cup from a fence-post, proved useful the first time he was jumped by rustlers outside of San Antonio.

His first gun was a Remington single-action revolver. The dark metal was pitted and the lead drifted right and downward regardless of his steady hand; but at close-range he was lucky that first time and the lead found its mark.

It had been an early spring night under the sharp stars with the wind pushing whispers through the tall grass and his horse nickering, restless, the brim of his hat pushed up and his thoughts on a pretty gal he had spied two days earlier when he smelled the greasy leather a moment before he was pulled from the saddle.

He was struck once and tasted blood. He fired from the flat of his back, straight into the chest of a man he could not see until the muzzle sparked and the black eyes dilated with a pain that faded as quickly as the heart his bullet shattered.

Four days later the same group tried it again and he wounded two of them. His reputation spread from that moment. Six months ago he stood down a group who objected to R.J.'s use of barbed wire and in the melee that followed Rafe shot another man. He was exonerated because the witnesses made it clear he was acting in self-defense, but Texas suddenly seemed a whole lot smaller. He was a target now; a game for any kid with a chip on his shoulder.

At R.J.'s insistence he made the ride to Wyoming with a letter of reference meant to smooth the way. He was disappointed in the marshal's reluctance — rather, his pointed refusal — to help him find work. But there was nothing else for him to do.

He would stay in town a few days

and see if he could find work on one of the outlying ranches. There was no hurry making up his mind to ride on. No hurry at all.

* * *

Rafe settled into a routine and spent the next few days looking for work, but the marshal's prediction of slim pickings was apparently based on reality. No ranchers needed help and the local shopkeepers didn't need a man with a reputation working for them.

The best way to learn things sometimes, he knew, was to listen; and the best place to listen were restaurants, church socials, or saloons. Having forsaken what he thought of as the phoney pretense of a churchgoer, Rafe was inclined to enjoy the tactile benefits of restaurants and saloons, the latter in moderation.

There were three restaurants in town and one boarding house that served meals. Rafe took his breakfast at the hotel each morning where he listened to the gossip about Mrs. Iverson's gout, Emmy Lou's pregnancy, and Deke Barlow's drunkenness. There was little change in his routine or the pedestrian knowledge he gathered; but after a time he fancied he liked the people of Twisted Oak well enough.

Bradbury's Restaurant offered the best meal in town, but the poorest gossip. All the same, Rafe was willing to chance an hour of lackluster eavesdropping in favor of steak and eggs followed by the best coffee he thought he'd ever had. One evening after his meal he was stopped by Bobby Shepard on the boardwalk. Rafe nodded politely and continued walking. He hoped to avoid a prolonged conversation. Bobby was a pleasant enough boy but Rafe planned on a few beers at the Valediction.

'How long will you stick around?'

'I don't rightly know. Long enough to get a feel for things, I suppose.'

'You find a job yet?'

'Nope.'

47

'I think the marshal's worrying some over Dutch Williams.'

'Why's that?'

'He's sent some telegrams he doesn't know I read, but I asked Mr. Curtis, he's the telegraph operator, I asked him about it and he told me. The marshal sent inquiries about Dutch and to find out if there's anything he's wanted for.'

'What did he find out?'

'Not a blamed thing! I think that's what's eatin' at him, too. He believes there's something going on but he doesn't know what.'

They were almost to the Valediction but Rafe slowed his pace. Bobby caught his interest after all.

'Where's Dutch now?'

'Nobody knows. But I'll tell you something else I know. There's hostile Indians out in the hills.'

Rafe stopped and examined the boy. His eyes were luminous and he seemed poised and alert. A kid with fancies of adventure, only just growing the first hair on his chin.

'Where did you hear that?'

'It was in one of the telegrams sent back to Ethan. There's been reports of cattle being taken from some ranches.'

Bobby said he had chores to do for Dan Haycroft. It wasn't much, sweeping up after last night's drunks, but the girls upstairs always tipped him a dollar each if he emptied and cleaned their chamber pots. He said with a sheepish grin, that Betty Anne sure was a looker. Then he was gone leaving Rafe to wonder about Indians and telegrams.

Later, after a few beers at the Valediction, Rafe overheard some men at one of the poker tables complaining that a few cows had disappeared, the general consensus being that a small group living in the hills was taking advantage of the local ranches. Indians were still a common sight but it had been years since any of them had shown any hostility.

At the end of the week he found himself on a first-name basis with some of the townspeople. He was treated respectfully, and only a few were reserved in his presence. He had learned a few things about Ethan, a great deal concerning the illnesses and ailments afflicting the population, but nothing that might materialize as employment. All the same, he was strangely content.

It was things he learned outside of not finding a job that stayed with him: the Indians were something to ponder, and the marshal's reputation for stubbornness, and the fact that two nights running in the Valediction he heard Dutch Williams referred to as an honest to God hot-blooded son of a bitch. The way things were shaping up the town was a powderkeg. Eventually someone would strike a match, either by happenstance or design. It was interesting to him the same way a man thinks it's interesting watching a mass of storm clouds build at the horizon. There was nothing to keep him in town, but leaving just now seemed premature.

Rafe pondered his dilemma. All he

needed was a job, some place to hang his hat while he sorted things out. One more day, he thought, then I'll ride up to Jackson Hole.

★ ★ ★

The following morning Amy O'Hara saw Rafe Morgan on the boardwalk when she stopped the buckboard in front of Grey's Dry Goods store. The young cowpuncher was the talk of the town, and she paused to study him. Something in his handsome, weathered face held her attention, then he looked her way and their eyes met. She felt a thrill inside of her and smiled, took a breath, swept her hand to her hair, brushing the curls aside.

Rafe returned her smile and started toward her. The moment seemed frozen as she watched him cross the street. She had been attracted to him immediately, from the moment she first saw him days before, and here he was approaching her again.

'Good morning, ma'am.' Rafe tipped the brim of his hat.

'Good morning, Mr Morgan. I see you're still in town.'

'Yes, ma'am. I'm looking for work. I was thinking if you knew of anyone in the area that might be interested in hiring me on.'

'I see. Well, first off, call me Amy. I'm Amy O'Hara.'

'O'Hara? Are you any relation to the marshal?'

'Of course. He's my father.'

Rafe had not known many instances where he was truly surprised. He swallowed and tried not to look perplexed. The marshal's daughter! He would have to walk carefully around this gal! Amy laughed and as if reading his mind she said, 'I suppose I should have mentioned it earlier. I'm certain my father had a sight more on his mind when he met you.'

'That's certainly true,' Rafe acknowledged. 'In any event, if you happen to hear of anyone that might need some help I'd be obliged if you mentioned it. Your father said there wasn't much work in these parts, but I thought I'd ask around.'

Amy pushed another drooping curl away from her brow. Her steady gaze revealed her interest. 'Well, it just so happens I might need some extra help, at least on a temporary basis. I'm not sure if I can afford taking on another hand permanently just now, but I'm willing to give it some thought.' A small pleasant laugh escaped her throat. 'I imagine it's something else I might have mentioned earlier when you told me you were looking for work.'

'Well, ma'am, if you don't mind my saying, I might be inclined to work for food and a bunk, at least for a couple of weeks until I see how things work out here. Keeping busy is the best thing for a man while he's sorting things out. I could use some time to put my thoughts together.'

Amy studied him, sensing his sincerity, and felt the last vestiges of caution slipping away as she accepted the fact this tall stranger excited her.

'Call me Amy. We don't have to be so formal. I suppose you might be useful for a time, although I don't know how you'll manage to get your thoughts together working for me. Operating a ranch keeps a person mighty busy.'

Rafe smiled again; that slow easy smile flashing across his sunburned face lit up his features, and in that moment Amy knew something that had never existed in her life before was becoming a reality.

'Is tomorrow too soon?'

'Not at all, Rafe — is it OK if I use your first name, too?'

'That's fine.' They both laughed a little nervously.

'My place is due north. You can't miss it.' Amy was thoughtful a moment. 'What's your full name, Rafe?'

'Rafael Morgan. But it's easier just to call me Rafe. My father married a Spanish woman and she named me after her father, but everyone calls me Rafe.'

'Well, Rafe, I wouldn't guess you had Spanish blood from your sandy-colored hair.'

'I expect not. I've been told my looks favor my father but my hot temper comes from my mother.'

'You don't seem so hot-tempered to me, and if you look like your father then he must be a handsome man.'

She thought a slight blush spread across his face, but then he was smiling again and the butterflies were loose in her stomach.

'They've been gone a long time now, anyway,' he said. Then he added quickly, 'Forgive my asking, but you seem awful young to be operating a ranch.'

Amy smiled. 'It was my father's place, our family home. After my mother died I sort of took it over.'

'I've always wanted a place of my own.'

An uneasy silence developed between them. Self-consciousness was not an O'Hara trait, but Amy was chagrined in realizing Rafe's steady gaze charged her with a self-conscious expectancy.

'It's been a pleasure talking to you, Rafe.'

'Thanks again. I'll see you in the morning.'

He tipped his hat again and left. Amy went into the dry goods store. She stopped inside the doorway and turned to watch him through the glass. The silence in the store seemed to pop in her ears. Her pulse was racing. She knew the clerks were watching her, but they could wait. A soft breeze snuck in with her and she felt the coolness of the store and the scent of oak and leather and linen; and she was aware of the nervous tittering of the two teenage clerks. They must have seen her talking with Rafe. The gossip would start now, but Amy didn't care.

My pa's going to be mad as a hornet!

She watched Rafe cross the street until he entered the hotel, and she lingered a moment observing the empty street where his boots had kicked up a little dust. A warmth spread though her body and she realized she was smiling.

★ ★ ★

The following morning Amy greeted him cordially and set him after Ben Wooley. 'Ben will set you straight on our routine here,' Amy offered, 'so time's wasting! We have plenty of work to do!' Her smile was dazzling. Rafe would have preferred a few more minutes of small talk but he wanted to impress this girl.

I should just stop thinking about that girl!

He told himself that very thing all morning. But it was no good. The marshal's daughter had gotten under his skin. He didn't quite understand the emotions that raked across him, but he didn't particularly mind it either. One thing was certain — for the first time in years he felt optimistic about his possibilities.

He felt good as he appraised the

ranch. The house was big, two stories, with plenty of windows that would catch the sun. The barn was almost as big as the house, and there was a second, smaller barn on the east side near the bunkhouse. The corral was expansive and delegated into sections for horses or cattle. She told him she had about two hundred head of cattle and that she sold most of it in the fall to buyers in Kansas. The fact that she was handling all this on her own impressed him. He found Ben Wooley in the bunkhouse. He was a tall man with a weathered face. His hair was nearly white and his eyes shone with merriment. Rafe introduced himself. They shook hands. Ben said, 'I heard about you in town.' Then Ben chuckled and said, 'That's all right. Some folks in town have nothin' better to do than spin yarns about a nice fella like you.' That put Rafe at ease.

'How many hands do you have to help out?'

'Two young Mexicans and a foreman

named John Gault who should be back in a few hours. He's away on personal business. Miss O'Hara hires drovers in the fall for the drive to Kansas. Gault keeps to himself. He's got a gal up in Jackson Hole, or so he claims. He should be back later. I don't care much for his temper.'

Rafe took Ben's comment as a salient warning.

'Sounds like you've had a few run-ins with him.'

'There's folks I know with a better disposition is all I'm saying.'

Rafe brought his bedroll to the bunkhouse and unpacked his ditty-bag of his few belongings. Taken with the clothes on his back, his chaps, a leather coat for winter his guns and his horse and saddle, they constituted his worldly possessions. And he had that thousand dollars in a money belt which he slid under the bunk mattress when Ben's back was turned. Rafe went out with Ben to look at the horses. There were six black horses in the corral along with Amy's mare.

'Broke two myself,' Ben said. 'They've got the spirit. They'll make good cuttin' horses when we move 'em down to Dodge.'

'The black I'm riding now didn't buck much when I broke her,' Rafe said. 'But she's a good horse all the same.'

'Some are like that, same as women, although a woman looks a sight better.'

Rafe chuckled with Ben. He was settling in, getting familiar with the place. He liked Ben and thought they would get along fine.

Near four o'clock that afternoon Gault rode up. He saw Rafe with Ben putting hay out in the corral for the horses. Ben introduced them. John Gault was tall and thin with dark features. A black stubble of beard peppered with gray shadowed his face. There was a scar on his face near his left eye which drifted down. This peculiarity in his eyes gave the impression he was never looking directly at you.

'There's talk of you in town,' Gault said.

'I imagine so.'

'You make certain you do what you're told around here. I won't tolerate trouble from a dollar-a-day cowpuncher.'

Rafe said, 'I'm just here to work.'

'We've got plenty of that to go around.'

In the early evening the two Mexican boys, Pedro and Jose returned from mending fences. They told Gault they had found damaged ones around the south rim of the property. Gault remarked they didn't look too slicked up from sweat and probably didn't get a damn thing done. He told Ben to take Rafe out in the morning and round up strays and when that was done they could start on those fences. Rafe figured Gault was a man who liked barking orders. Well, he was welcome to it. Rafe would do his job and give the man no reason for complaint.

Amy did all the cooking in the big

61

kitchen in the ranch house. She served them all a fine beef stew thick with tomatoes, onions, some venison and small potatoes. There was fresh bread to go with it, plenty of coffee, and afterward Amy surprised them by serving a steaming tin of apple pie. Ben rolled his eyes and grimaced as he held his stomach. 'I don't think I can handle much more,' he said with his gaze fixed on the pie. 'You have yourself a time up in Jackson Hole?' Ben said to Gault.

'Time enough,' Gault said, never raising his eyes from his plate. 'Sorry I missed all the excitement.'

Ben shot a glance at Rafe.

Amy said, 'I expect Rafe here will help us get things shaped up right quick. There's those fences to fix and strays to find.'

Gault was silent, but Rafe sensed the man was feeling threatened by his presence. He would have to build his confidence with these people over time. And he had time now, plenty of it.

Thanks to Amy he had time to prove himself useful, time to plan some kind of future. He made a mental note to ask if she had a safe in the house. A thousand dollars under a bunk mattress could prove tempting to someone hard up for cash. He figured Ben might be all right about it, but the Mexican boys were young and impetuous. No sense tempting them if they should discover the cash. And Gault had a surly edge he didn't trust. He was going to take no chances.

There was no further talking at the dinner table. As was the custom among ranch hands, they forked down their food and when finished rose, took their hats from the pegs near the door, offered a polite thanks to Amy, and went out to finish whatever chores waited before sunset.

After dinner Ben went out to the bunkhouse with Jose and Pedro while Rafe and Gault checked on the horses. In a little while Rafe heard singing and laughing. Amy came off the porch to join them as they walked back from the barn.

'Ben has a good voice for singing,' Amy said, 'Why don't we go listen for a while.'

The men were comfortable with Amy in their presence and Rafe was pleased Ben and the two boys treated her respectfully. The two Mexicans were very young, possibly no older than twelve or thirteen, but Amy said they were both capable and loyal. It was obvious they were taken by Amy's beauty and competed for her attention.

Ben played an old guitar and sang cowboy songs late into the evening. He smiled and chuckled and stammered along when he forgot the words, but nobody noticed or cared. He sang sweetly about the lonesome prairie and then he sang rowdy songs that made everyone stomp their feet. He sang about the gold rush and lost loves and forgotten fortunes, his hands strumming the guitar gently, his foot tapping out the beat. Even the usually dour

Gault sat on his bunk watching silently, his foot tapping to the rhythm. Amy and Rafe danced, their boots kicking up dust on the planked bunkhouse floor while Jose and Pedro clapped their hands, joining Ben on the chorus. The night was filled with the sounds of cowboys singing and they did not stop until the stars were burning in the velvet sky for many hours.

Much later Rafe followed Amy back to the ranch house, allowing himself a moment's reflection as the cool night air filled his lungs. 'Thank you for everything,' he said quietly.

'Goodnight,' she said. She turned and looked at him and before he could say another word she spun on to the porch and was gone, leaving him only one last brief smile before shutting the door.

By the time he walked back to the bunkhouse Ben and the two Mexican boys were all snoring soundly. But Gault's bunk was empty. Curious, Rafe stepped back outside and walked over to the corral. Sure enough, Gault's horse was missing. Where would he go at this hour? Rafe tried to dismiss his suspicions. Gault might very well have needed a drink and gone to town to fill his belly in a saloon, but Ben had clued him in about Gault and Rafe's instincts told him things weren't right. Still, it was too damn late to worry about it now. Reluctantly, Rafe turned in hoping he'd have a better feel for things in the morning.

3

Dutch Attacks!

'What do you mean you hired him?'

'I mean what I said, Pa, I hired Rafe Morgan and he's working at the ranch.'

'Good Lord! Have you lost your mind?'

'Don't use the Lord's name in vain.'

Ethan was tongue-tied. He looked around his office absently, struggling to comprehend what his daughter told him. Eventually he said, 'That's a hell of a responsibility to take on without consulting with me.'

'I didn't know I needed to consult with you. Why are you upset about this?'

'He burned Dutch Williams as bad as he could.'

'But you said that wasn't his fault?'

'It wasn't his fault, but the point is

67

Dutch will want a piece of him now. The healthiest thing for Rafe Morgan to do would be to ride on.'

'I don't understand? Why should he ride on? If Dutch starts any trouble you can put him in jail.'

Ethan frowned. There was a point where arguing with his daughter was useless, as was the case with her mother, and Ethan never expected to win an argument with a woman.

'We don't need to get riled up about this,' he said, trying to change his tone. 'I'm only saying you might have asked my advice first, that's all. No harm done. Now that you have the facts it'll be a simple matter to tell him you made a mistake.'

'A mistake!'

She was glaring at him, her hands on her hips, her face red with anger. There were times when Amy bore a striking resemblance to her mother, a fact Ethan noted more often lately. When she was angry her mother's hot temper flared to life and Ethan was looking at a ghost with astonishment as well as remorse. Mary's untimely death left a void in their lives and he missed her counsel and pragmatism. She would have known how to handle their hot-tempered daughter, but the best he could hope for now was to amble into things with his usual stubbornness.

'He's dangerous,' Ethan said. 'He has a reputation. It's the kind of thing that gets every tin-horn sod-buster in the territory into thinking he can make a name for himself by taking on a fast gun.'

Amy shook her head. There were times when her father's stubbornness was too much to bear. They had been arguing only a few minutes, since she walked into his office after picking up her supplies from the hardware store. 'You said there aren't any posters on him, so how can you compare him to a gunfighter? You're not making sense!'

Now it was Ethan's turn to shake his head. The exasperation was evident in his voice. 'A reputation is just as bad as

69

being a gunfighter. All it takes is some pup with a gun . . . ' His voice trailed off. There was no point in belaboring the issue. He knew he could never talk his daughter out of something once she had made up her mind.

'You worry too much,' she told him, throwing her head back, her hands on her hips defiantly. The movement was not calculated on her part, but in that instant Ethan saw again his dead wife and he was struck by a feeling of deja vu. Ten years earlier Mary had used the same words when Ethan voiced his concern about balancing his duties as a deputy US marshal with those of a rancher.

'I'm only asking you not to be so headstrong,' he urged Amy. 'Take a moment and think about things. Maybe you'll change your mind and see things in a different light.'

'I would think there are more important things for you to be worrying about, especially if worrying is all you can do.'

The sarcasm was heavy in her tone and Ethan felt the fight slip out of him. He cleared his throat, fiddled with the papers on his desk.

'We'll see if this brash cowboy is worth all the trouble.'

Amy appraised her father in silence. He might have told her then about the rumours surrounding Dutch Williams but her defiance — even her strong-headed individuality — impressed him, although he wasn't about to admit it. And she was right about him worrying too much. He would do all the worrying, he decided, and keep an eye on Rafe Morgan at the same time.

Amy ran her hands through her long red hair and shifted her gaze away from her father. A moment of uneasy silence developed between them. Ethan felt a pang of guilt as the color flushed in Amy's face.

'I'll be in town Sunday to take care of some things. We can ride back to the ranch together. I'll let you know how Rafe is doing then.'

She slipped out the door before he could say another word. He got up from his desk and watched her from the window. Very much like her mother, she captured a man's attention with her natural beauty. Nature would take its course, Ethan knew, and there wasn't a damn thing he could do but hope for the best.

The sun was dropping and the town was filled with a soft peaceful glow that Ethan knew was a temporary feeling, although he tried to enjoy as much of it as he could. Ethan hadn't told anyone that a drover passing through had mentioned seeing a camp of heavily armed men just five miles east. It had to be Dutch.

Ethan was pensive. Trouble had come to town again in the form of Dutch Williams and his gang. Maybe more trouble than he could handle. In the past he'd deputized volunteers only as the need arose, but too often there were no volunteers. Few men wanted to play second fiddle to a marshal with a reputation. He took pride in his position as a deputy US marshal, but it was an unenviable job. There was just too much territory to cover.

He had a Winchester, a Colt, and the stubbornness he was born with to stand against a dozen men.

★　★　★

On Sunday Rafe and Ben did their chores after breakfast and within the hour Amy came out of the house in a new calico dress. Standing there on the porch in her new dress, and with the sunlight tangled up in her red hair, Rafe thought he had never seen a woman so beautiful. The thought crossed his mind he should ask her to marry him right then. A moment ensued where Rafe and Amy stared at each other without moving, both smiling without realizing it, until Ben politely coughed and said, 'I've got the buckboard ready.'

Gault, having returned early that morning from another overnight trip to parts unknown, declined the invitation to join them. Rafe thought the man seemed agitated but the sight of Amy in her new dress quickly occupied his thoughts. Amy rode the buckboard into town while Rafe and Ben followed on horseback. Amy wanted to go to the Sunday church service before taking care of any business. She seemed disappointed when Ben and Rafe declined but didn't press the issue having learned to leave men to their ways. Ben said he wanted a belt of good whiskey and they started for the Valediction Saloon. Amy instructed Rafe to meet her at the bank where Bobby and her would wait for him after the service. Then they would deposit Rafe's money. He had told her about the money the night before and she insisted that he do the sensible thing and open an account. 'Your money will be perfectly safe,' she'd told him.

They had not been in town ten minutes when Rafe noticed a man against the post outside the Valediction.

A thick set Mexican wearing twin bandoliers across his chest and an ivory-handled Colt on his right hip. The cartridges in the bandoliers gleamed like metal teeth. He was leaning against the post and casually smoking a thin cigar. He was one of the men who had chased Rafe and fought with him in the dark street after he burned Dutch. Rafe felt those small, dark eyes appraise him from beneath the shadowed brim of a black sombrero.

'That's Carlos Duranos,' Ben said.

Rafe studied the man, but the Mexican was already feigning disinterest. He concentrated on his cigarette and only briefly looked at Rafe again with those brooding, obsidian eyes.

Rafe and Ben went across the street, up onto the boardwalk next to the Mexican, and pushed through the batwings into the Valediction Saloon. They stood in the doorway a moment letting their eyes adjust to the darkness. Rafe was conscious of the silence that suddenly enveloped him, and the sounds he heard outside — a wagon rolling through the dust or the monotone conversation of pedestrians strolling along the boardwalk — seemed far removed from him.

The Valediction was empty save for Dan Haycroft who stopped scrubbing a table and looked up at them.

'Good morning, gentleman.'

'Something to kill the weasel,' Ben said.

Dan poured two small glasses of his best whiskey and set them on the oak bar. Rafe stepped up and drank half the glass.

A board creaked and a turning spur tinkled like soft music outside the batwing door. Rafe squinted at the sunlit doorway where the Mexican's silhouette floated into the saloon. Duranos eased up to the bar next to Rafe, his spurs clanging against the brass rail.

'I don't want any trouble in here,' Dan said.

'No trouble. Just whiskey.' Duranos

never looked at Rafe or Ben.

Dan poured a glass and moved down the bar. Rafe knew he still had the shotgun down there, under the oak bar near the gleaming spigots. Dan did a good job of pretending to polish glasses, keeping his hands low.

Duranos knew it too. He sipped his whiskey, keeping his hands visible, sipping slowly as he savored the warm alcohol.

Duranos smacked his lips. 'Whiskey is good for clearing the dust from a man's throat.'

Duranos studied Rafe in the mirror as he struck a match and lit a cheroot. Both men watched each other's glassy reflection.

Duranos examined the burning matchstick.

He twisted the match in his hand and snuffed out the flame between his thumb and forefinger. He finished his whiskey and turned to Rafe.

'We never finished our fight.'

'Maybe we can finish it sometime.'

Rafe wasn't about to let himself be intimidated.

Duranos flashed a yellow toothed grin and shrugged. 'It is your choice, amigo.'

The Mexican spun the glass down the length of the bar toward Dan. 'I still don't like your whiskey.'

They watched Duranos slide into the sunlit doorway, push out into the street, his boots thudding on the boardwalk.

Rafe drank the rest of his whiskey while the echo of the Mexican's thudding boots faded away. Ben, who had already motioned for Dan to pour him another, drained his glass and said, 'Dan, you gotta stop lettin' the riff-raff in here.'

'He's been hanging around all morning.'

'You seen Ethan around?'

'He's out there. You know him. He doesn't miss anything.'

Rafe sipped a second whiskey. He wasn't the type to get drunk, and he wasn't about to let himself get lazy with drink while that Mexican was hanging around. Amy had his thousand dollars in her satchel and after church they were going to the bank together. He wanted to get that over with, and then see what Ethan O'Hara had to say. He hadn't seen the marshal since taking the job, and Amy's assurance there would be no problem did little to ease his mind. He had to face the marshal on his own terms, let the man have his say.

Ben was on his way to a long day having already made it clear he would stay in town overnight and let loose a bit. The whiskey was going down quick and easy and he smacked his lips with appreciation as Rafe took a small sip.

'Church won't let out for another thirty minutes,' Ben said, 'then all the ladies'll be jabberin' outside like chickens. We better stay in here and keep out of sight.'

Another drink finished and Dan had another ready. Ben made the drink disappear and said to Dan, 'Hell, just leave the bottle.'

'What do you suppose that Mexican is up to?'

'That greasy polecat? He's struttin' is all, showin' his feathers.'

'I think he means trouble today,' Rafe pondered. 'I'd better go see the marshal and let him know something is up.'

'Ethan's got this town locked tight,' Ben said. 'I expect he's ready for anything.'

'All the same, I'm going.'

Rafe left the Valediction as Carlos Duranos rose from his chair on the boardwalk, stretched and yawned, flicking a drifting fly away with a lazy sweep of his hand. Duranos started walking down the street. He kicked at a red hen pecking at some scraps in the dust. Rafe was watching from the boardwalk outside the Valediction. It appeared to him the Mexican had waited for him before starting down the street. Duranos tossed a sickly smile at Rafe before turning on his heels and heading away. He disappeared into the alley between the hotel and the dry goods store.

When he came out a few minutes later his hat and gun and bandolier belts were gone. He had rolled up his sleeves. Duranos lifted a thick hand and waved for Rafe to come.

Rafe was curious but not surprised. He was heavy, but shorter than Rafe. His eyes held a wicked expression both of malice and amusement. The look on the Mexican's face told Rafe everything. The Mexican was confident and prepared.

Rafe held back a moment, making his decision. Ethan was nowhere to be seen. He glanced at the marshal's office down the street. A curtain flapped in the open window but he didn't see the lawman. That the Mexican wanted to fight was clear, and his motivation as Rafe saw it was to settle what they had started that night in the dark street after he had burned Dutch Williams. If he settled it with the Mexican now that might defuse any trouble. After another glance at the marshal's empty office,

Rafe went toward the alley.

Duranos stepped forward and jerked a fist into Rafe's face. Rafe ducked and countered with a right, but Duranos was fast and also ducked the punch. A greasy smile broke across the Mexican's face. 'I am not wearing a gun, *amigo*, so why do you?'

'All right,' Rafe said. He unbuckled his holster and set it on the fence.

Duranos piled into Rafe and both men rolled over in the dust and bounced back to their feet. Duranos landed a fist across Rafe's forehead. Another blow caught Rafe on the chin and he staggered. When Duranos stepped in for another strike Rafe sidestepped and drove his fist into the Mexican's ribs. Duranos cursed.

Rafe landed another right, this one on the side of the head, and Duranos lunged into Rafe's midsection. The two men grappled briefly until the Mexican forced Rafe deeper into the alley. They rolled inside the shade between the buildings.

Duranos swung a powerful right and clipped Rafe on the jaw. But Rafe's punch was faster and his knuckle bruised the flesh under the Mexican's right eye.

'That is nothing, *amigo*!' Duranos sneered. 'Come closer and try me again!'

Rafe stepped in and caught Duranos on the mouth with another right. He saw the Mexican's lip split and a berry of blood roll down his chin. Duranos wiped his mouth with his sleeve. He gestured for Rafe to come closer.

Rafe had an instant of realization of how he'd been duped before John Gault stepped up and struck him on the head with an axe-handle. His skull exploded with pain. He was on his knees suddenly, clutching his bloodied scalp. Duranos was laughing.

'This one has a hard head,' Gault said.

They lifted Rafe to his feet and the other man held his arms. Duranos peered closely at Rafe, flashing his yellow teeth as he grinned at his victim. The punch caught Rafe in the ribs. He felt the balled fist strike a bone and the breath was forced from his lungs. Before he had time to draw another breath he was hit again.

'Give the son of a bitch a lesson,' Gault said.

Then the outlaws went to work on Rafe. They tossed him between them, bouncing knuckles off his head as he teetered back and forth. Rafe threw his arms up to protect his face as both men struck him at once and he went down again. Dust filled Rafe's mouth. The pain shot through him like a hot iron.

They kicked him several times, sending bolts of pain through his body. When they stopped he heard a distant thundering but it was difficult to concentrate through the veil of pain.

'Dutch is gonna be glad to see you,' Duranos grunted.

They tied his hands behind his back and Duranos went to work on him, pounding Rafe with his fists and kicking him viciously in the ribs. Finally, Duranos buckled on his guns and fired two quick shots into the air. The shots were a signal to Dutch, but even as Rafe realized this he was sinking into the depths, the speckled blackness closing around him.

★ ★ ★

Ethan had in fact been watching as his daughter rode into town with Ben and Rafe. Carlos Duranos, had come to town early and took a place near a post outside the Valediction, smoking quietly and watching the street. Ethan studied the stocky Mexican carefully and concluded he was a formidable opponent.

The Mexican was restless. Sometimes he leaned against the post and just watched the street. It was these times, when Duranos was on his feet, that Ethan expected trouble. But most of the time Duranos sat on one of the old chairs on the boardwalk with his sombrero pulled over his eyes pretending to sleep.

Ethan returned to his office and checked his guns. It was a habit he developed in the war when his rifle jammed from the sand in the breech. Keep your damn guns clean. He ran a cloth over the cold metal of his Winchester and sat with it across his lap as he waited. Goddamn it, they had to pick a day when his daughter was in town. This might be nothing though, he thought; maybe they're just stretching it out, trying to get a feel of the possibilities.

But Ethan knew they were up to no good.

The coffee was running through him like water through a worn goatskin. He knew it was due to nervousness, the way he couldn't hold his water anymore, and age. After relieving himself Ethan went through the back of the jailhouse, past the cells to his office and saw Carlos Duranos had left his place on the boardwalk. A few minutes earlier, Duranos had gone into the

Valediction but had come out again just as Ethan was about to walk down and stop any problem between the Mexican and Rafe Morgan.

He stood outside his office and surveyed the street. Nothing much was happening. Most everyone was in church, including his daughter. Rafe and Ben were undoubtedly still in the saloon. Those shopkeepers not in church were in their stores.

It wouldn't hurt to walk to the Valediction, stop in, make sure that burly Mexican wasn't causing trouble. Whatever they were up to, Ethan aimed to stop it.

It was ten o'clock and the morning service was over. He turned his head and saw the crowd begin streaming from the church. In a moment he saw his daughter with two women walking along the street, talking amiably. Turning his head in the opposite direction he saw the empty street.

He couldn't wait any longer. Something was up and he had to know what was happening. Another glance at the churchgoers. Amy was nearing the bank. She stopped and seemed engaged in conversation with those two women. She hadn't looked in his direction yet. He thought if she saw him she might come in his direction. Turning quickly, he went up the street.

Ethan had not walked twenty paces when he heard two gunshots from an alley further down the street. Immediately two riders cut out between the buildings at the end of the street. They saw him and the shoulders of the two riders dipped as they pulled their guns.

Ethan had started down the street without his rifle. He'd left it on his chair when he went out back to relieve himself. Cursing, he pulled his Colt and fired before either man could get off a shot. Ethan's shot missed but the maneuver enabled him to sprint from the street and crouch behind a balcony post on the boardwalk. The riders reined their horses and Ethan snapped another round of hot lead in their direction.

That should keep them worried a moment, he thought.

At the sound of gunfire the crowd on the other end of the street dispersed into various buildings. The two riders had backed their horses into an alley on his side of the street. He couldn't see them but he could hear the nervous shuffling of hoofs, the creak of saddle leather.

The gunshots had come from the opposite alley. Ethan waited.

Duranos and Gault came out of the alley with Rafe between them.

Ethan never hesitated. He jolted into the street fanning three shots at Duranos. Still running, he turned and fired again and ran like hell across the street. Ethan had enough confidence with a six-shooter to know he could avoid hitting Rafe, but Duranos was faster than he thought. The Mexican spun easily on his heels as Ethan's gun came up. Duranos darted down an alley. Gault slapped his gunbutt across Rafe's head and followed the Mexican. Ethan was running but his legs were like lead.

I'm getting old, he thought, I haven't the wind I used to have. Duranos and Gault had disappeared. Ethan stood with his back flat against a storefront and thumbed cartridges into his gun. He took several deep breaths. The riders in the opposite alley had wisely moved out of sight.

Now, goddamn it, before they can think about it. Ethan swung into the alley.

Duranos and Gault were nowhere to be seen when Ethan ran into the alley. He found Rafe propped against a fence, his head bleeding profusely. He heard the pounding of hoofs as he was lifting the groaning cowboy to his feet.

Bullets ripped through the air as a rider galloped around. He emptied his six-gun into the alley. It didn't matter that he missed. Ethan was pinned down and Rafe was out of the action. Ethan felt despair wash over him. They'd succeeded in making him look like a fool.

Then the rest of the Dutch Williams gang went past in a rush, the hoofbeats thundering along the street and echoing off the false fronts of the unpainted buildings. Ethan eased Rafe into a corner and crawled up toward the street. His heart sank as he saw a group of men brandishing six-shooters enter the bank.

The first explosion shook the town.

Another group of Dutch's men had ridden in two abreast firing their guns haphazardly to minimize any retaliation. Ethan felt the anger flare to the surface when he saw some of the outlaw gang tossing dynamite. They blew open the bank and went in while the other men circled the street blasting away with their guns and tossing the dynamite at the storefronts.

Ethan was numb with astonishment and anger. The outlaws' destructive actions were born out of greed and an

91

ignorance as to the value of human endeavor. The outlaws lit the fuses with their cigarillos and sent the lethal sticks whistling into the air. The street reverberated with the echoes of explosions. The very earth shook from the tremendous detonations.

Ethan pulled Rafe deeper into the alley and tried to position himself to get off a shot. Rafe was groaning but it would be a while before he had his senses back. He saw Adam Washington down the street at the livery firing at the outlaws with his Winchester. Two riders came up fast on their horses and emptied their guns in the livery. Ethan saw Adam sprint back into the shadows and knew he would be able to cover himself from the blacksmith's barn that adjoined the livery, but they had him pinned down.

A explosion took out the hotel balcony.

The street was in bedlam.

Ethan's vision was obstructed now by smoke and dust. For a moment the world became a cacophony of sound; the quick, hard burst of blasting caps ripping open the storefronts; the endless whinny of frightened horses and the shrill cries of the outlaws.

Dutch and his men were ripping apart the town like hungry wolves. Six men were left on horseback to keep the people at bay, and they did so with a deadly earnestness. They flanked the street, first using their Winchesters or six-guns and firing at anything that moved. If nothing moved they sent their hot lead through windows and doors. The exploding dynamite was the death knell and they let it ring loud and clear. The sizzling sticks whistled through the air, clattered against the shake roofs and blew the clapboard into sawdust.

Ethan went around the building and pulled himself over a picket fence. It wasn't easy for him to lift his weight onto the rickety fence and for one sickening moment he thought the wood would give way under his weight and send him crashing. But he managed to get himself over although the effort tired him. The blood was pounding in his temples and he cursed the fact his mouth was dry.

His intention was to circle around and come out further down the street, nearer the bank, and fire upon the outlaws before those in the bank mounted up and made their escape. A dog watched him with mild interest, its tail lazily swishing away flies.

He was ten feet away when the dog suddenly looked to its right, down the alley toward the main street, and Ethan saw the hair come up on its back and its nose twitch. The dog rose to its feet, keeping its nose low and sniffing, as one of the outlaws emerged from between the buildings on horseback and flung a sizzling cord of dynamite at the beleaguered US marshal.

Time seemed to stop as Ethan watched the dynamite cartwheel in the air before he felt himself running, but much too slowly. The detonation sent a shock wave ripping through the alley and he tumbled to the ground, his hands clamped to his ears. A geyser of dirt erupted with a cloud of dust which mingled with the debris shaken loose from every shingle and board along the alley. In the seconds it took him to hit the ground and make a quick mental assessment that he was uninjured, he turned on to his back, drew his revolver and fired once through the cloud of dust that hung in the warm afternoon air like a heavy blanket.

His shot missed and the horseman was gone. A shower of dirt sprinkled across his face and the detonation's echo boomed in diminishing waves until all that remained was a trilling in his ears. I need one good shot, he thought, and then another. He hugged the wall and ducked his head for a fast look.

Through the smoke and dust he saw the outlaws leave the bank. They tied the money sacks to their horses and hustled into their saddles. They mounted quickly and spurred their horses into the street. When they passed Ethan he saw Dutch Williams pause, reining his horse and glaring into the alley where the marshal was poised.

Ethan felt a jolt of shock crash over him as he looked at Dutch. The man's face was seared red, the skin blistered and mottled with sores.

A group of riders came up alongside Dutch. They had Amy and Bobby on horseback, their hands bound behind them. They were bracketed by Duranos and Gault. Amy's eyes were wide and frightened, but she looked at her father and a resolve crept into her eyes.

Dutch glared at Ethan and said, 'Bring the man who burned me or these two will die.' Then Dutch sighed. 'Maybe they will die anyway.'

Then they were gone in a gallop, a swirl of dust in their wake.

4

Pursuit

Adam Washington was waiting at the livery. The tall black man stood framed in the doorway. He had known Ethan O'Hara longer than anyone else.

'I'll need help on this one,' Ethan told him.

'Goes without saying.'

'There's reports of Indians, maybe Sioux and Arapaho, and even Cheyenne.'

'I ain't deaf. I've been listening to people hereabouts complain about Injuns for some time now. But I don't like that part. I don't like Injuns.'

'I want you to find Black Wolf for me.'

'I don't trust Injuns, but I'll find him. When you leaving?'

'As soon as I get supplies together.'

Adam pulled a thin cigar from his shirt pocket and lit it with the scalding poker he had resting in a small fire near the bellows. After a moment he said, 'It sounded like the battle of Hatcher's Run out there today. They had me pinned down pretty good.'

'They won the day. That's a fact.'

'Been a long time since I thought about it. Those boys had some gumption about them. All that popping in the air today made me think none of that war really goes away. It keeps coming back, and those outlaws out there today are just part of the same fight.'

'I don't think about the war much.'

Then Adam said, 'They're using Amy as bait, setting you up.'

'I expect so.'

'I best be getting on then.'

Ethan nodded. 'Just find Black Wolf.'

★　★　★

It took Rafe and Ethan thirty minutes to gather provisions. They loaded a pack horse with hard tack, flour, coffee, bacon but mostly boxes of .45 cartridges for the Winchesters and the Colt six-shooters. Their concern over Amy and Bobby was kept in check by their preparations. Thirty minutes was a long time for Rafe as he helped gather supplies. The marshal hadn't said much to him but he knew he blamed him for all that happened. When they were ready they mounted their horses and started down the street. For Ethan it was no different than going to war but Rafe was conscious of people watching them. People lined up on the boardwalk watched them as if they were trying to remember it for later.

Ben joined them and said the ride would sober him up. During the attack he'd tried winging a few shots from the saloon entrance but the volleys of gunfire kept him and Dan hunkered down behind tables.

The three riders cleared the grasslands along the river and began the long ascent into the hills. The timberland was flooded with an undulating light, divided by the dark canyons and snow-capped mountains of the west.

Rafe Morgan sat astride his saddle and surveyed the faint trail they had found an hour earlier. As expected, the outlaws were making no effort to conceal their tracks. They followed the hoof marks and horse droppings along the river until the trail turned west into a hilly range of ponderosa.

They followed the trail through swales and gullies wary of an ambush for all three men understood the danger they faced. Five hours later they halted a few minutes to rest the horses before moving on. Ethan squatted on the ground looking for sign.

'Here,' he said, 'there's more sign. They stopped here like we have and sent a rider out, probably to check their back trail. They're in no hurry.'

'Let's get on the trail then,' Rafe said impatiently.

Ethan frowned. 'We'll need these

horses as fresh as we can keep them. We'll rest here awhile.'

For a man who had his daughter kidnapped the marshal sure had a lot of self-control. But Rafe was inclined to trust Ethan's judgment for the moment. Rafe and Ben dismounted and studied the landscape with Ethan. He calculated the time they had traveled with the time elapsed from the robbery and tried to determine how far Dutch Williams had gone.

'What do you think they'll do?' Rafe asked.

'Their trail is consistent,' Ethan said. 'They're traveling only fast enough to keep us at a distance. They want us to follow into those slopes, up into that high country. Amy is the bait. They know I'll come. That's where they'll be waiting, up in those rocks.'

Rafe glanced up at the hills and said, 'We get up into those hills and you can hide an army in those canyons. A man could get lost for years and never find his way out.'

'Not to mention the Indians,' Ben said wryly.

They moved on, letting the horses canter along an animal trail. An hour later they left the trail and turned south-west into the heavy timberland. They talked little and the only sounds were the occasional creak of leather or the faint crackle of hoofbeats on the pine needles. There were a few sycamores and oaks scattered along the ridge. They circled north. Ethan wanted to come out on higher ground for a better look.

The mountain sloped up steeply, like the broad shoulders of a slumbering giant, and they could see the buff-colored cliffs that dispersed into serrated ridges towering above the verdant timberland. As they moved closer the mountains reminded Rafe of a castle, a dark old fortress throwing its long shadow across the meadows and valleys.

They rode deeper into the forest, skirting the rim of the battlemented cliffs. The wall of mountains circled westward and after a while Rafe had a sense he was being watched. He knew this was not foolishness, for he was an experienced trail hand and long ago he recognized that the sensation born from his instinct was true. They expected a trap at some point and Rafe preferred an attack sooner than later. He knew that once a man was engaged in the heat of a battle all fears were diminished and his actions then were animated by instinct and skill.

Ethan took out his old army field glasses and scanned the canyon for signs of life. Still none of them had spoken and Rafe knew an uneasiness had been following them like a vengeful ghost. A bird called from somewhere among the tall grass and Rafe spotted a deer grazing calmly near the trickling stream. Despite the tranquil setting, their horses were nervous, their ears pricked, listening.

'Dismount,' Ethan said softly. 'Take the horses back and find cover for a camp.'

Without a word Rafe and Ben walked the horses under cover of the trees and found a space on the far end of a thicket where a campfire at night wouldn't be visible from the canyon or the far cliffs. They unsaddled the horses and let them nibble at a ridge of grass nearby.

They made a rough camp and rejoined Ethan at the tree line overlooking the verdant basin. They were on a ridge about sixty feet from the valley floor. Off to their left was a trail leading down toward the stream. They couldn't ask for better cover, and they could take any possible direction to escape an attack.

An image of Amy came to his mind and he was momentarily overcome with grief. Such a beautiful girl at the mercy of a monster. If anything should happen to her . . . He took a breath, trying to control his emotions. Ethan glanced at him, almost as if he were reading his mind, so Rafe stared straight ahead, tight-lipped, jaw set firmly in what he hoped was a determined look.

Ethan had said Amy was the bait, so she would be alive long enough for Dutch and his men to spring a trap. The idea was to avoid any ambush and get Amy back. He had to trust Ethan who believed the girl wouldn't be harmed. Probably, he thought, she was alive but treated roughly. Such men as Dutch Williams would have no qualms about abusing her. He wanted the opportunity to make the outlaw pay for this injustice. Initially, Rafe had felt a pang of guilt at the burning of Williams's face, but the attack on Twisted Oak and abduction of Amy served to instill in him an unyielding hatred for the man.

'Dust.'

Rafe followed Ethan's gaze. Dust rose like vague spirits dancing along a far trail near a balustrade of cottonwoods. The dust came up past the trees and dispersed above a rocky hogback. Then they saw more smoke to the left of this.

'Indians,' Ethan said, 'coming this way.'

Rafe studied the rocks in the distance. The dust followed a switch-back and dipped into the valley. After a few minutes he could see the dust was nearer and he could make out the figures of Indians on horseback. And something else.

Some of the Sioux had rifles and many were armed with a bow and quiver of arrows. Rafe noticed most wore buckskin pants which led him to believe they made their camp in the high country where it was cold at night even in summer.

'This is a determined band of Sioux,' Ethan said.

'It's a war party,' Ben said. 'They're looking for two-legged game.'

The Sioux drifted out into the meadow and brought their horses up to the stream. They were less than a hundred yards from the posse crouched in the trees on a ridge above them.

After a while several Sioux mounted

and rode off, circling dangerously close to the hidden men before turning off to the left. Presently, the rest of the war party followed along the same route, circling below them and moving on toward the south-west. One brave cantered his horse away from the war party and looked up at the ridge where the three men were hidden. The men edged back behind the tree line even though they knew they weren't visible at this distance. But an Indian's senses are finely honed and the three men waited patiently as the brave studied the landscape. If a horse whinnied their location would be revealed. At last the brave rode off.

The Indians were well armed. Rafe had fought Indians before and respected their ferocity, but he knew that if they were discovered here they held an advantage with the high ground from where their rifles could wreak havoc on the Sioux. They watched the Indians with fascination, a tight grip on their guns.

'They look to be making a methodical search and swinging back into those hills,' Rafe observed.

'That's trouble for more than us,' Ethan said. 'Let's go.'

They mounted up and followed Ethan along a narrow trail. That night they waited on the ridge without a fire. Ethan said it was too dangerous a risk. They ate biscuits and beef jerky and drank some water from their canteens.

Fear and uncertainty were feelings that had to be controlled. Telling himself this, Ethan tightened his resolve, letting his fear slip down into a dark place where he held it fast against a current of emotions. He knew what could be accomplished through stealth and cunning. He knew that Adam and Black Wolf were his ace in the hole. There was a chance of separating Amy from her imprisonment although he had no idea how this could be accomplished.

The afternoon light faded swiftly and they prepared a quick meal. Darkness crept out from the trees and rocks and filled the forest with black shapes. Their food was eaten by the time the sky faded into blackness.

'We'll take shifts on watch,' Ethan said. 'The last shift should be about an hour before sun-up and then we move out.'

'You think those Indians are trailing those outlaws?' Rafe asked.

'More than likely. Better them than us.'

'It didn't seem they were on a specific trail,' Rafe commented. 'They were looking awful hard, but their pattern was methodical, and they were circling that valley searching for sign. I heard Custer is up in Montana and there's been Indian trouble since he came out of the Black Hills.'

'Custer's a damn fool,' Ethan remarked. 'He had no discipline during the war, but he liked to have his picture made and see his name in the paper.'

They were silent for a moment, each lost in his own thoughts.

Rafe asked later, 'What exactly are you planning?'

'I think Dutch and his men circled this valley before heading west again into the mountains. Dutch and his gang know we're here, but they don't know where. I aim to keep them guessing. If we're careful, those Indians won't realize we're here. If we do this right we get my daughter back.'

'I'll take the first watch,' Ben offered.

Ben's watch was uneventful. All he saw in three hours were a dozen deer gliding through the starlit grass like pale, brown ghosts. He fought off sleep but the stress of following the outlaws had taken its toll. Near the end of his watch his eyelids were drooping under the weight of exhaustion. He was grateful when Rafe relieved him.

'You do what Ethan says and you'll be fine,' Ben said. 'Don't question him because it'll just make him angry. If you talk too much you'll remind him you're around and make things worse.'

The old wrangler appeared self-assured and in control. Rafe saw a sincere man trying to help, offering advice like a father would.

Rafe's watch was also uneventful, with the shining difference that he was consumed by a sense of guilt for all that had befallen them. He thought glumly that things had gone wrong from the moment he burned Dutch Williams and it looked to take a great deal of work to fix it. But this thing he started would be settled, and no outlaws or renegade Sioux would stand in his way.

He was apprehensive as the hours of his watch dwindled away. The night was still and the valley was bathed in starlight. The long silver grass rippled in the breeze and the stream tinkled along reflecting the spangled arc of stars. The mighty constellations shimmered and swept slowly across the horizon. He saw many deer cross the stream, stopping only briefly to drink. He loved this country with its wild beauty. He thought about Amy and felt his heart go

111

out to her. He was responsible for her plight and felt both anger and guilt that his actions had resulted in her being harmed. The few days he spent at the ranch had changed him. He had known many women but this one was something special, a woman a man might attempt anything for.

Rafe had remained silent about the Indian threat, but he was inwardly dismayed at the odds against them.

Ethan relieved Rafe a few hours later and Rafe fell asleep instantly. When Ethan woke him after several hours he felt he had only crawled under the blanket moments earlier.

'Anything?' Rafe asked.

'Nothing,' Ethan grunted. 'Antelope and rabbits. Get your gear together. We ride in fifteen minutes.' Ethan began saddling his horse.

Rafe saddled his horse and then retrieved his Henry rifle from against a tree stump where he'd left it. He wiped off the morning dew from the barrel with his bandanna while letting his peripheral vision watch for movement. He was about to mount his horse when he saw movement across the valley.

Far off, near an alleyway of ponderosa, he saw the dark shapes of birds suddenly flip into the air, circle on the wind and take refuge in the trees further to the right. It happened in mere seconds.

Something unseen was there, and all that remained was to find out who or what. The birds might have been startled by an animal, a deer or possibly even a bear, but Rafe didn't believe it. His instinct told him different and he studied that grove of trees for a few more minutes but there was no further movement.

'You need to hurry it up,' Ethan said irritably.

Rafe pointed out where he saw the birds rise from the trees and Ethan studied the spot with his field glasses.

'Nothing now, but we'll be careful there later. I think there's a higher trail that crosses over that place and might offer a view if it's trouble.'

Ethan handed Rafe the glasses and he studied the rock formations. There was an indication of a ridge running parallel above those trees. It was worth exploring.

'The Indians change everything,' Ethan said. 'I hadn't figured on so many, although I knew they were in the area. What worries me is that there may be more. Once Amy's safe we take on Dutch.'

'Those Indians looked to be hunting and they seemed real intent on their business.'

'I don't want them to find Dutch first, but I don't see any way around it. Those men have been leaving sign for our benefit and the Indians are tracking them now.'

'It doesn't exactly make sense, though, seeing those braves all riled up. I'm no expert on Sioux, but they're stirred up about something. They have to know the men they trail are heavily armed and even an Indian wants to stay alive.'

'But it's an Indian's way to count many coup against his enemies. Anyway, we'll have to wait and see.'

There was still snow in the highlands but the days were hot and the snow was melting. The sky was clear and when the sun retreated behind the rocky crest it was only cold in the high country where the wind carried a sound like that of an old chief whispering around a campfire.

5

The Madman

Amy O'Hara looked into the face of a monster and made a silent vow she would kill him. He was a powerful thick-bodied man with fingers thick as sausages. She winced when he touched her. His face was horribly burned and parts of his flesh were infected. There were a few wisps of black and gray hair left at his temples, but the rest of his scalp and face were blotched with scabs and blisters. The skin under his feral yellow eyes was mottled like a cobweb, and when she first saw him at the bank she thought for a moment he was wearing a grotesque mask.

Dutch and his men had brazenly entered the bank with guns drawn and helped themselves to as much money as they could fit into their saddle-bags and

116

sacks. She was worried about Rafe. He was supposed to meet her at the bank but he was late. They took the satchel containing Rafe's money. Angered, she stepped up and said, 'What in God's name are you men doing? You have no right to come in here and take our money!' But before she could utter another word a Mexican backhanded her, sending her sprawling. She was unceremoniously forced to her feet by the foul-smelling Mexican. The memory of his lingering hands filled her with anguish.

When she fell her head grazed a chair. When Dutch noticed the teardrop of blood he said, 'Be careful with her. She's a pretty one.' He finished filling a sack with money from the teller's cage and said to the Mexican, 'Bring her with you. I have uses for a pretty hostage.' Bobby, who accompanied her, was taken as well. When Bobby had bravely rushed to Amy's defense Dutch had pistol-whipped him. She feared the boy was seriously injured. She was

117

relieved later when he opened his eyes and tried to smile at her.

John Gault set his eyes on Amy and said, 'She's the one I told you about, the marshal's daughter.'

That was the first time she had noticed Gault. She looked at him but he wouldn't match her gaze.

Dutch Williams looked at Amy and said, 'All the better.'

The ride had been a nightmare. Her head ached terribly and the Mexican's grip was like iron. They rode all night, and their pace was so furious she was certain the horses would drop from exhaustion. A few hours later they picked up their remounts and proceeded with another furious ride across the countryside.

The outlaws had come across the Indian camp after daybreak and she watched in horror as Dutch and his men slaughtered the helpless Sioux. She had never seen such a ghastly scene, had never dreamed that men could be so cruel and merciless. It was obvious the men were gone or there would have been more activity. One boy was left behind; he was gathering kindling for a fire a hundred paces from the circle of tepees. They took the boy prisoner, then surrounded the camp. When his men were in place it was a simple matter of opening fire. A few volleys from their rifles and it was over. For Dutch it was like shooting chickens in the coop back home in east Texas when he was a boy. Dutch laughed when he saw them scrambling around in fear, cluck-clucking in mindless agony. Sixteen dead Indians.

After it was over Amy vomited in the grass and whimpered and struggled against the ropes that turned her skin purple at the wrist. Then Dutch bound her mouth with his bandanna and in her terror she bit her lip. When a little blood trickled down her chin Dutch pressed closely to her, never taking his eyes from hers, and licked the blood clean of her flesh.

Her flesh was salty and tasted good.

He thought she would faint but the girl had courage. She was repulsed by him and that made him feel like a man. He cupped her breasts and squeezed.

Young and supple. Just the way he liked them.

Dutch pressed two fingers to Amy's face and traced a line down her cheek. Her flesh was flushed pink, like a pale rose, her eyes clear like the morning sky. A truly beautiful woman. And she was revolted by him. It was there in her eyes, visible in the lines of her face.

Revulsion.

Now Dutch Williams took out a knife and held it before the Indian boy's face and said something. He was talking to the Indian and turning the knife slowly in his hand, letting it catch the sun. She couldn't hear what he was saying. His voice was low, almost a whisper, and she didn't believe the Indian understood him.

Then, with a quick and silent thrust, he plunged the knife into the Indian's chest. She heard the hard sound of the blade striking bone and a sound like air leaving a bellows. The Indian grunted. Dutch held the knife in his chest, standing close and staring into the dying boy's eyes, then he twisted hard, forcing the knife into the heart.

She was trying to scream but it was muffled by the gag.

Her muffled screams sounded like the faded whimpering of a wounded animal remembered dimly in a dream. She squeezed her eyes shut and refused to watch the horror unfolding before her.

The fear and exhaustion had taken its toll until finally she slipped into merciful unconsciousness. Later she was pushed firmly and pulled to her feet. One of the riders, Ellroy, was trying to have his way with her. He smelled of whiskey and stale sweat. His eyes shone with lopsided intoxication and his breathing came in wheezing gulps as he pulled at her clothing. She was jostled like a sack of potatoes. She couldn't speak. She couldn't scream. It was too much and her eyes filled with tears. She could feel Ellroy's rancid breath slipping over her, feel his saliva dripping on to her face. She tried to lash out but she was firmly bound. Her coat was being torn from her.

Dutch Williams appeared above her, a misshapen beast towering above their grappling forms. He lifted a rifle high in the air and brought the stock down on Ellroy's head. Ellroy yelped and crawled away.

'The pretty one is mine,' the monster said. 'You touch her again and I'll kill you.'

Ellroy cursed and moved away clutching his bloodied head.

Amy faced her captor with a trembling she could not hide. The other men were nervous from the killing of the young Indian, but offered no threat to Dutch Williams. They would follow his orders because he had made them rich. But killing the Indian disturbed them, and some of the men talked low amongst themselves. Sometimes they stole lustful glances her way, and she knew she was spared a rape only because they feared this disfigured outlaw.

'My father will be after you,' she said to Dutch Williams.

'And he will find me,' Dutch said.

'Yes, he will, and when he does you will have more trouble than you can handle,' she said emphatically.

Dutch Williams was serene. A calmness came over him and his hand came up to his face, gently tracing the blisters and peeling skin. The skin on his left cheek twitched as his fingers caressed an inflamed spot.

'I'm looking forward to it,' he said.

6

Black Wolf

The Shoshone called Black Wolf emerged from a strand of aspen to sit on a boulder and observe the valley below.

He sat quietly on his rock, comfortable but alert. Black Wolf was a patient man and now he was waiting for the next omen. There was much activity in the valley. He watched the furthest ridge where the three riders made their camp.

In the mountains to the north a dozen riders fled the Sioux. They were led by the tall man with a burned face. Black Wolf had no doubt the Sioux would take many coup from these men. The white men were foolish in not covering their trail. Death would claim them as his own for the House of Darkness.

The white man with the burned face was a poor leader. He could not possibly survive and the killing of the Sioux brought him closer to the firepit of the Dark House. Black Wolf knew the blood of many men would run into the earth and the Sioux would make a victory dance near their corpses.

He surveyed the landscape and recognized the possibilities. The distances to be traveled and the direction of the men culminated in death for many when they came together. The three riders camped on the ridge would have opportunity for survival. They were cautious and moved with ease in the forest. He knew one of these men, Ethan O'Hara, by his horse. This man had courage and would make a fine battle if he was to die. The Shoshone admired men with courage.

Ethan had sent a rider to seek him out, as he had before, and Black Wolf watched patiently as the tall black man moved up the trail.

He waited patiently for several hours,

watching the black man's progress through the lush landscape. He ran his eyes across the dark woodland. He venerated the familiar sounds of animals scrounging for food and the dip and sway of trees dancing in the wind. This was his home. The old ways were diminishing as the number of his people dwindled, but long ago Black Wolf had chosen a solitary path that suited his temperament. He followed his chosen trail without regret.

An image flashed through Black Wolf's mind: the first time he had met the black man they called Adam they were camped down in the valley. Black Wolf walked up behind Adam as he sat with Ethan at the campfire. Black Wolf asked Ethan to share his coffee and Adam jumped to his feet and complained he was scared half to death to hear a voice behind him in the dark. You're never alone, Black Wolf had told him, but the black man acted as though he didn't understand.

When Adam Washington rode closer

he detached himself from the rock and stepped into the clearing.

Now Adam saw Black Wolf standing in the moonlight.

'You make a lot of noise,' the Indian said, 'but you are difficult to see at night.'

Adam flinched at the sound of Black Wolf's voice. He looked around, satisfied they were alone, and dismounted. Adam said, 'You've probably been watching me for the last two hours, taking your sweet time about it while I tire out my horse getting here.'

Black Wolf was silent. His features were impassive like that of the carved oak chief outside the tobacco shop in Cheyenne.

'Ethan sent me. His daughter's been kidnapped and we need to get her back.'

'It will cost you many blankets, cartridges, and a horse.'

'What the hell you need another horse for?'

'You will give me a horse.'

'What happened to the last horse we gave you?'

'You will give me another horse.'

Adam shrugged. He knew from experience there was no sense arguing with a stubborn Indian. He went to the rock where Black Wolf had waited and surveyed the valley.

'So where are they?'

Black Wolf came up beside him and pointed. 'There on the far ridge in those trees are your friends.' He pointed north and said, 'The men you seek are higher in the rocks. There are Sioux in the valley, not far from the place where you crossed to find this trail.'

'We should meet up with Ethan in the morning.'

'Perhaps. The burned man attacked a Sioux camp and killed many. Now the Sioux will have vengeance.'

'Dutch attacked them! God Almighty, that man's insane!'

Black Wolf shrugged. Adam knew there was talk among the Indians at Fort Laramie that Black Wolf was an outcast medicine man. There were those that said he communed with the dark gods of the mountains. Others said he was a half-breed and could find no peace among the Shoshone or white man, so he roamed the high country, a man who belonged only to the wilderness.

There was nothing to do now but wait until morning. He took his bedroll and made a place next to the cliff wall. He unsaddled his horse and left him picketed in the trees. Adam announced he was hungry and fetched biscuits and beef jerky from his saddlebag. He offered some to Black Wolf. The Indian shook his head and said he would make a fire in order to cook a rabbit stew.

'We can't have a fire up here, any damn fool knows that. Those boys see us and it's over. Not to mention the fact there's Injuns a lot less friendly than you roamin' around.'

Adam felt insulted when Black Wolf said he could make a fire that was undetectable to anyone watching from below. The damn Shoshone always had a better way or a better idea, and it irritated the hell out of Adam.

'Go ahead then,' he said. 'If you've got such a mind to show off I won't say another word.'

Black Wolf built a small fire under a pot and waited for the water to boil. When the pot was steaming he took a rabbit he'd caught earlier and skinned it, diced up the meat and added it to the pot with some of Adam's biscuits and a few small potatoes.

When the concoction had simmered about forty minutes he separated it into bowls. Black Wolf sat on his haunches and slurped it down. Adam hated admitting it, but the makeshift stew was delicious. The fire hadn't attracted any attention, and Black Wolf had succeeded in showing him up again.

Black Wolf asked for tobacco and Adam gave him the pouch. He packed the tobacco into a thin pipe carved from buffalo bone and handed the near-empty pouch to Adam. He said nothing further and went off to smoke by himself.

Adam knew the Indian had his own ways about him, and there was no sense guessing what he was up to.

Black Wolf was true to form, and when Adam was asleep the Indian took a roundabout route up the trail. It was a beautiful night with the brush of stars visible through the dancing aspen leaves. He had lived long in this place with many victories over his enemies. He might die soon but it would be a good death and many would follow him to the House of Darkness.

This land was changing, had changed so much already since his youth. Now the white man held dominion over all, but there were battles yet to come before all the tribes were defeated.

He rode on a trail known only to a few, a trail that took him higher, and near the outlaws' hidden camp. An hour later he was on the perimeter of the camp. He had reached a rise in the rocks overlooking a small basin thick with ponderosa.

The breeze carried the scent of their coffee and the echo of their voices.

Leaving his horse, Black Wolf went over the rocks. Some of the trees were very close to the cliff and without hesitating he grabbed a branch and swung out into the darkness. His movements were graceful and silent and he had taken to the tree effortlessly. He hung from the branch, letting his eyes adjust to the darkness, then he carefully pulled himself forwards.

He edged to the other side of the tree where he had a clear view of the camp. A dozen men were bedded down around the campfire. The woman was next to the fire, her hands tied. He thought she was sleeping. Two men were on the far side in the forest, about thirty yards apart, standing guard. A few of the men around the campfire were awake and talking in low voices. Their speech reminded Black Wolf of the low, guttural grunts of tired pigs rooting around a mudhole.

The camp was not situated in a good place. They were lucky, he thought, because if the Sioux found them there was no escape. They had backed themselves against a wall and a quick, forceful attack would destroy them.

Black Wolf had seen such stupidity in white men before. If he survived, a good warrior learned from his mistakes, but so many white men were not good warriors. The white men had taken the land from his fathers not with a warrior's skill, he knew, but with brute force. These men were all the more dangerous because they were stupid.

A slight movement brought his gaze on the man with the burned face. His eyes gleamed in the firelight. One of the other men near the fire turned to him and said, 'We need to be sharin' that woman. We ain't had no sportin' with a gal in a long time and we oughta take her now, all of us, one at a time.'

'You'll do nothing until I say.'

'Don't seem right,' the other man said.

The burned man lashed out with his fist. He was very fast and Black Wolf admired his speed and strength. His fist hammered into the man's mouth sending a splash of blood across his lips. The man howled and fell back.

Then the burned man was on his feet, holding his gun at the man's head.

'I'll kill you,' he hissed, 'and any one of you sonsabitches touches her, I'll kill you.'

'It just don't seem fair, you havin' your way an' all.'

Another fist rocked the man's head. He was knocked unconscious and when he fell over his arm flopped in the fire and began to burn. Nobody moved.

Dutch Williams quickly dropped his gun in the cradle of his holster and stepped back. He looked around at the men. A few were looking at him, and a few pretended not to notice what had happened.

The unconscious outlaw came to a moment later and jumped to his feet and howled, slapping his arm to smother the fire. The campfire threw shadows across Dutch's face and for a moment it looked to Black Wolf as if the fire still burned beneath the outlaw's skin.

'You got the money from the bank and you can buy all the sporting gals you want in a few days,' Dutch said.

Thirty minutes passed and there were no further incidents. Black Wolf waited until he thought most of them were sleeping before climbing down. He went down quickly but silently, like a shadow falling through the trees.

He paused on a low-hanging branch and peered at the ground. Down a slope and through the greenery, a quick left and circle around. He would stand near the guard. He could do this silently.

He made his move. There was no noise as he rushed across the slope. As he moved he was conscious of the shape of the lone sentry. Black Wolf reached a midway point and froze. Now he examined his surroundings again and made slight adjustments to accommodate his new knowledge of the terrain.

The man on his left was furthest from the cliff. He would have to go back up the trees and ascend the ridge to escape. If they were alarmed to his presence they would naturally consider the attack from the opposite side of camp. He was confident they would never suspect someone climbing down the cliff-face.

He could feel the darkness, warm and enveloping. But there was substance beyond the inky veil. His fingertips found his knife and he struck quickly. The man was standing on the opposite side of a bush when Black Wolf jolted through the air, the blade sweeping at an angle. The Indian felt the warm blood jettison across his knuckles as the blade swept across the guard's throat. The man's arms flailed for a moment, clawing the blackness, and he dropped to his knees. Something whispered in the night, a last breath taken in the darkness before his blood poured down his chest, soaking his knees, staining the grass at his feet.

The dying man exhaled; a faint whisper and nothing else. Before the man stopped twitching Black Wolf retreated into the foliage and remained motionless, listening.

There was another guard fifty paces away and he turned as if he might have heard something. Black Wolf watched him knowing the guard could not see him. When the figure resumed its relaxed posture Black Wolf moved again.

He was up the trail and ascending the tree quickly. The dead guard would be discovered at the change of watch, if not sooner. They will panic, he thought, and waste energy chasing ghosts.

Black Wolf had taken the first blood. Now the battle would become heated, but taking first blood was a good omen. He retraced his path through the trees, climbing up through the branches, inching along the limbs, feeling his way intuitively in the dark. He scampered on to the ridge and found his horse.

The night was still and unmoving. He found a small rivulet between some rocks and let the cool rushing water wash the blood from his hands. He cleaned his knife and took his horse again down the trail. He sang a war chant celebrating his encounter, his chest swelling with pride. He might continue his harassment of the outlaw camp if the girl were harmed. He remembered seeing her as a child at Ethan's ranch when his wife was still alive, a small bundle of energy and happiness. Ethan valued her life more than his own.

He let his horse pick its way through the gray shapes of trees, down and around the hill until he was near the ridge where Adam slept.

The stars had begun their slow fade but it was still dark when he returned to the camp to find Adam sitting up in his bedroll.

'Where the hell were you?' he asked.

'I went to the outlaw camp. The woman is alive. I killed one.'

'You killed one of them?'

'The burned man follows a trail of death,' Black Wolf said.

'You crazy damn Injun!' Adam grunted. Then he rolled over and went back to sleep.

7

Rendezvous

An hour before sunrise the posse followed the trail along the valley's perimeter. Two hours later they rested the horses. They were silent, keeping the horses calm and staying under cover of the tall trees whenever possible. Once the sun was up they had to rest the horses frequently. It was another hot day. They were alert for sounds and half expected an ambush.

The trail was wide and well-worn. Again and again Rafe's thoughts reverted to Amy. He was foolish, he thought, to think of her so often. He certainly had little to offer such a woman. A roving gunfighter had no future outside of a shallow grave without even a Christian marker.

He could leave the wandering days

behind and try to make something of himself, maybe start a ranch with some good cattle. That would be a start, he decided. There had been enough years caring for other men's cattle. But primarily he thought about Amy; a solitary image in his mind that he wouldn't let go.

They had gone up the trail another hour when Adam Washington came out from behind a tree with a Winchester cradled in his arms and said, 'You guys make more noise than a wounded reb hollerin' for his mama.'

Rafe had his six-gun out.

Ethan said 'Don't. He's a friend.' He frowned at Adam. 'Where's your horse?' Ethan asked.

Adam nodded over his shoulder and said, 'Just up the trail a bit.'

'And Black Wolf?'

'He disappeared a little while ago. He's like a damn shadow moving round these woods. He told me I'm to take you up in those high rocks and he'll meet us there.'

Rafe looked at Ben. 'We started out with three and now we're four.'

'Five if you count Black Wolf. Gives us better odds,' Ben said.

'Who's Black Wolf?' Rafe asked.

'An Injun friend of Ethan's,' Ben said. 'He takes some getting use to.'

Rafe wondered why Ethan hadn't said anything about this black man and an Indian friend. But still, it made their chances a sight better.

'There's one more thing,' Adam said. 'Black Wolf killed one of the outlaws, and he told me Dutch and his men encountered Sioux in the valley.'

There was stunned silence for a moment before Ethan said, 'Lead on, then. I expect this trail to get mighty crowded soon.'

Adam led them to the left of the main trail, along a slight incline and deeper into the underbrush. At one time it might have been an animal trail, but it didn't seem used now. At least there were no deer tracks. After a while it didn't appear as if they were riding on a trail at all.

For a long time they traveled downhill into a maze of lodgepole pine and spruce. They rode silently and Rafe went over all the events carefully, considering every aspect of their situation. The appearance of Adam Washington was a surprise and the mention of an Indian named Black Wolf was equally surprising. So Ethan was a man who planned things more than he liked to admit.

And if Black Wolf was a friend of Ethan's and somehow managed to kill one of the gang then the odds might be swinging in their favor. But where was the greatest danger? Possibly the Sioux. They were the variable no one had planned for. At least twenty Sioux, maybe more. And Adam said Dutch and his men killed some Sioux, so they were out for vengeance.

They would have to try to get the girl back and escape the Sioux as well as Dutch Williams. Rafe's mind was crowded with the problem and he tried to stop thinking. He tried concentrating on the beauty of the forest or the gleam in Amy's eyes, but thinking about Amy made it more difficult. Another few days of riding, he thought, and he'd be up in Montana in a bunkhouse, or joined up between here and there on a trail drive, and not riding through the shade of pines while being chased by angry Indians. Not riding like this into a trap set by a madman with a burned face. But that wasn't right either. Nothing was right about it. He couldn't run. He owed the marshal something. And Ethan had planned well, after all.

Rafe thought about Amy again and the way her eyes shone with merriment and the soft curve of her figure. She was something to think about. There was no getting around it. Of course there was nothing to think she might be interested in him, and the West was never short of men with money and influence who might court such a pretty girl. But oddly, the fact he had nothing to offer made him all the more eager to prove himself in some way.

They proceeded cautiously and made their way up the incline until they were directly over the lower trail. They were almost across the valley and near the place where he'd seen the birds stirring. Ethan had been right and they found a narrow path that led up into the rocks overlooking the trees.

From here they could see the trail below. A dozen birds flocked around something and he caught a glimpse of reddened flesh. His heart sank.

'We have to go back down and see for ourselves,' he said, and before the others could respond he was moving down the trail. At the bottom they followed a switchback and rode into the trees.

The breeze brought them the smell before they were close enough to see it. Birds flapped into the blue sky and their warning whistles mingled in the air with the smell of decaying flesh.

They had gone a hundred yards when they came upon the birds. They were in a swarm, pecking at something stationed in the center of the trail. They were black birds and their beaks were flecked with red strips of flesh.

Lashed to a sapling branch was a severed human arm. All but the index finger were pushed down to the palm. The hand pointed the way up the trail as insects and birds made breakfast from its flesh.

'Dutch wants us to go this way,' Ethan said.

★   ★   ★

Below them in the long valley the sun glinted on a rifle barrel. Ethan turned to Rafe and said, 'Sioux.' Rafe watched the movement in the long grass. The Indians were on their trail, coming up rapidly behind them. Another thirty minutes and the Sioux would reach the place where they had found the first hand.

They found the left hand a little further up the hilly trail, pointing the way.

Ben said the two hands belonged to an Indian and Adam agreed. The skin was dark and the palms calloused. They speculated how Dutch and his men might have hacked them from a body. It was a ghastly sight and Rafe was visibly shaken.

'Dutch Williams has a lot of balls to attack an Indian camp,' Ben said.

'He's a damn fool,' Ethan responded, 'but even a fool can be dangerous.'

Ethan looked at the hands and they all knew what he was thinking.

'What kind of devil cuts up an Indian like that?' Adam said.

'One that doesn't fear God,' Ben replied.

At this height Rafe could see beyond the valley where a small lake sent whitecaps toward a distant shore and the glare of the sun reflected against the buttes and a faint haze softened the view.

They rode slowly, careful to make little noise, alert for sounds. Ethan took the lead with Ben and Adam following.

Rafe ambled in the rear, watchful of any movement from behind.

After another hour their horses were sweat-slicked and breathing hard. Ethan called them to a halt and Adam warned they were still in danger. He had a place in mind where Black Wolf said they would be safe and they needed to keep moving.

'There's nothing we can do,' Ethan said. 'These horses need rest or they'll drop beneath us. We'll hole up here. Rafe, you and Adam set up post on our back-trail.'

So they made a camp as the dust shimmered in the heat. When they were situated Rafe and Ethan spread out along the base of a cliff, keeping to the shade when possible while Adam watched the trail for signs of pursuit. The men were impatient but Rafe knew the marshal had made yet another wise decision. Both men and horses needed rest and Rafe knew Ethan wasn't about to let themselves run ragged.

After a while Rafe said, 'So you got a

plan to handle his ambush when it comes?'

Ethan said, 'I need to see what it is first. I want to look at it. Something like that I need to look at. Once I see it maybe I can see a way through it.'

'It might be too late then,' Rafe said. He gazed upward at the not so distant ridges. Dutch Williams was setting a trap, and he would do it there, in those sun-bleached boulders. Rafe's guess was that Dutch would make his move soon, unless he had failed to avoid the Sioux. Rafe lifted his hat and wiped the sweat from the hatband, gazing off again at the ridges.

In a little while Adam came back and sat in the shade next to Ethan.

'Being outnumbered bother you any?' Rafe asked.

'I'm going to get Amy back, and bring Dutch Williams in to hang, or kill him, whichever seems best at the time.' Ethan's voice had risen in pitch and his eyes flashed like blue steel.

'You always did have a stubborn

streak.' Adam pursed his lips thoughtfully. 'Killin' is something we're always up to.'

'We're good at it.'

Ben, thinking it was time to change the subject, looked at Adam and said, 'Seems to me I heard you been doing more than one kind of hunting. What was the name of that freckle-faced whore you were hankering after?'

'Ruthie's her name.' A smile flickered across Adam's face. 'She can twist a man into some kind of knot. The Mexicans call it *El pequeño muerta*, dying a little death.'

Ben chuckled. 'There's worse ways for a man to die.'

'Anyway, there's always a fight,' Ethan said. 'None of us can run from that.'

Some time later, when Ethan was out of earshot, Adam said to Rafe, 'You can trust the marshal.'

'I trust him, but I can't exactly figure him out.'

'There's no sense in trying to figure a

man out if you trust him. I've known Ethan a lot of years, and I don't understand him, but I sure trust him.'

'How long have you known him?'

'Since the war.'

Rafe looked at Adam. He was tall, well over six feet, Rafe estimated, and immensely powerful. His brown skin was smooth and unblemished and his eyes were dark and penetrating. The stubble on his chin, seen from a distance, seemed like a dark scar that added to his fierce looks. Here was a man not to be trifled with, and there was a keen intelligence lurking in those eyes. He was the kind of honest man Ethan would have as his friend, and the level of trust Adam demonstrated toward the marshal was reassuring.

'I met Ethan somewhere around Petersburg in early '65, I think,' Adam continued. 'I was a young buck in the Twenty-fifth Corps. I was separated from the brigade when a musket ball grazed my head. One minute we're advancing on those wily rebels and the next I'm face up on the grass watchin' clouds roll by, except they weren't clouds, it was gunsmoke. I didn't even know I'd been hit. There was yellin' and screamin' all around and I remember wishin' everyone would all just hush so I might get me some sleep. But the screamin' continued for a long time.'

Adam leaned against the cliff wall and looked up at the sky. 'Some time later a man appeared above me; it was Ethan, and somehow he got me back to camp. They told me later I had three bullets in me, two in the side. The bullet that skimmed my head dazed me and when Ethan came along he saw a rebel stop and fire two rounds at me. Ethan said it was the way a man will stop and shoot a helpless dog, but Ethan saw I was alive. He killed that reb with his bare hands.'

The two men were silent a moment, lost in their own thoughts as the afternoon shadows stretched across the rocks. Then Rafe said, 'I'm glad I came along, although I'll tell you part of it is guilt because I feel responsible.'

'The way I see it, Dutch and his boys were out for trouble before you burned him.'

'I know, but maybe they wouldn't have taken Amy.'

'Bad men like that don't need reasons for what they do.'

8

Battle

Adam rode behind Ethan, followed by Rafe and Ben. Rafe watched their backtrail. The body parts discovered along the trail had unnerved them, although they didn't speak of it again. Their pursuit had become something more than an effort to retrieve the marshal's daughter. Ben's usual wise-cracks, usually greeted by laughter, were now met by polite, hollow laughs that amounted to mere whispers.

Sixty yards away, at the base of the mountain wall, a tunnel had been dug for mining. There were still several wheelbarrows nearby. One was resting near the tunnel entrance, loaded with rocks; another was overturned a few feet away, the wheel broken. There was a shovel and pick lying in the dust near the tunnel entrance. Such abandoned mines were common, most of them having given up little in silver or gold, and the efforts worked here were of men who struggled vainly for riches the earth held secret.

They were not alone. When they entered the clearing Rafe's horse snickered and threw his ears forward. His nostrils flared and he stomped a hoof.

Propped on a post at the tunnel entrance was the severed head of an Indian. The eyes were rolled back and the mouth was agape, swarming with flies. A plank of wood was nailed to the post beneath the head, and written on this with charcoal from a campfire were the words: WELCOME POSSE.

Amy was tied to a post a few yards from the mine tunnel. Bobby was thirty feet away, tied up and propped against a rock. He looked defiant, but relieved to see that help had arrived. The wind blew her red curls in Amy's face. She was gagged and blindfolded and her blouse had been unbuttoned by Dutch Williams who stood next to the tunnel smoking a thin cigar. He smiled when they looked at him.

A hail of gunfire erupted and they reared their horses back as .45 slugs slapped the canyon walls. They retreated out of range behind an outcropping of rock as Dutch Williams let loose with a peal of laughter that sounded like the screeching of a vulture.

They scrambled for cover, retreating to a thin copse of pine.

'Four or five high up on the left in those boulders. The rest below. Two or three near the mine entrance,' Ethan said, his hard gaze studying the landscape.

He dismounted and walked along the rock wall. He looked out at the mine. They read it in his face when he turned around. He was ready. He pulled his Winchester from the saddle boot and levered a cartridge into the chamber.

Ethan went back along the boulder and watched without speaking. Adam and Ben dismounted as well and walked along the rock wall until they could see what Ethan was looking at.

Rafe looked at Ethan. The tall lawman was already scanning the area with his eyes, picking out the other outlaws, trying to make as quick an assessment as possible. Rafe looked around but he couldn't see anyone else, but all the same, he knew they were there. He edged his horse forward.

No one moved.

'She is very soft, my friends,' Dutch said as he walked over to Amy and caressed her chin with his left hand. 'She's soft like a baby, but she screams too much. I think I should cut her tongue from her head. Did you know a woman's tongue is good to eat? This may surprise you, but I assure you it's true. A woman's tongue cooked over a campfire will fill a hungry man's belly.'

Still Ethan didn't speak.

He was watching Dutch carefully now. The horses were nervous from the smell of blood and the flies that seemed to be everywhere, swarming in the air. Their horses snickered, flicked their tails.

'I don't hear you talking to me, my friends, and after such a long journey I thought we could talk and be friends.' Dutch swept a hand across Amy's breast and squeezed. When he touched her body jerked against the rope that held her and a muffled groan escaped the gag in her mouth.

'You see how she is? I had to gag her because she wanted to scream. This is so annoying. If somebody doesn't talk to me soon I'll have to kill her.'

The anger buried in Rafe broke open like fire licking up from ashes, flaring to life and eager to feed.

'You killed one of my men the other night,' Dutch said. 'That was a foolish thing to do. Did you think that would scare me? The death of a man standing guard in the dark isn't heroic.'

Dutch pulled a knife from his belt and smiled again and in that instant Ethan said, 'Get her back,' and Rafe had the gun in his hand and fired in one movement that occurred so swiftly Dutch was taken by surprise. The first bullet clipped the rocks to the left and then the outlaw was diving for cover as Rafe spurred his horse. He emptied the six-shooter as the loud, angry snap of rifle fire ripped at the rocks around him.

Dutch might have died on the spot if not for the strategic placement of riflemen in the high rocks. They kept the posse pinned down and stitched a line of holes in the dirt as Rafe sprang into view. Ethan and the others fired as quickly as possible to cover Rafe.

He dropped from his horse with his Colt in one hand, a knife in the other. The thought flashed through his mind he wasn't fast enough and it was just luck he hadn't been hit as he cut Amy from the post. She collapsed to the ground and he cut loose her gag and blindfold. She looked up at him with frightened, tearful blue eyes and he said, 'Don't worry,' when the rifle fire cut down his horse. The horse reared, whinnied in pain, and collapsed, thrashing on the ground, a gout of blood splaying from the hole in its back. Before the horse finished thrashing Amy had rushed past Rafe to pull the Henry from the saddleboot.

She fired as quickly as she could jack the lever, popping rounds at the riflemen in the rocks. The intensity of her actions took Rafe by surprise.

'Save your shots,' Rafe said. 'They've got us pinned down here. Let's get back.'

Now Rafe could see where the others were located, all up in the rocks circling the mine entrance. He saw a rifle barrel high above and heard the crack of splintering rocks as a bullet flattened itself against stone. He was forced to move into the mine entrance, almost dragging Amy with him.

'Don't worry,' he said again. Amy crouched behind him, brushing the tears away from her face. She took a breath knowing she had to calm herself.

'You did good coming for me,' was all she said.

Rafe reached back and gently touched her shoulder. Her blouse was moist and warm from sweat and he felt a tremor run through her. 'You'll be fine now — ' he started to say as a bullet clipped the rocks on his left. He returned his attention to the view from the mine. He glanced at Bobby. The boy would have to wait. Bobby locked eyes with Rafe and Rafe nodded, a silent signal to let him know he'd be back for him. Bobby nodded back.

A burst of gunfire sent them scrambling for cover deeper into the enormous cavern.

'All we have to do now is find a way out of here,' Rafe said.

⋆ ⋆ ⋆

Ethan and the others had immediately taken cover. Ben was busy returning fire with his rifle. 'Save your ammunition,'

161

Ethan ordered, 'they made it to the mine.'

They had watched Rafe spur his horse forward in a brash move that resulted in him freeing Amy but pinning them down in the mine. There was gunfire after the outlaws pursued them into the mine shaft, and then silence.

There was a shelf of rock fifty feet across that shielded them from the persistent fire from the outlaws. Adam and Ben were off to the right about thirty yards away, guarding the only accessible perimeter. It was a stand-off.

When the firing began the acrid smell of gunpowder filled Ethan's nostrils and he was in Virginia again, running at the rebel line. The air filled with dust and the whining sound of bullets and terrified whinny of horses in panic.

He pulled his hat brim down over his eyes and squinted up at the hills. Most of the outlaws were up there, rifles picking out of shadows among the rocks, hoping for a ricochet. He had a glimpse of Duranos near the mine. Maybe three others with him.

Where had Dutch gone?

The outlaw had disappeared when the gunfire began. Ethan wanted to believe he was wounded, possibly dying, but he knew it wouldn't be that easy.

'*Amigos*! You are very foolish. You think we don't know what you are doing?' Duranos bellowed. 'You think you can outsmart us? Please, my *gringo amigos*, throw down your guns. You have nowhere to go.'

Ethan levered a round into the Winchester, picked a spot above the mine entrance, and fired. The bullet slapped against the rock sending up a small puff of dust. Some rock fragments rained down near the mine, close to where Duranos was hiding. There was a hearty laugh from that area.

'Very good, use the ammunition. I can wait to kill you sonsabitches later.'

Duranos stuck his head out and looked at them. He was smiling. Ethan wanted one clean shot at the bastard. He was smiling like he knew something. He had a lot of brass. Adam and Ben hunkered down next to Ethan.

'He's a happy snake, isn't he?' Ben said.

'Acts like he's got us all tied up,' Adam grunted.

'Let's split up and circle around,' Ethan said. 'If we can get around those rocks we might get a better view.'

They heard a boot scuffle against stone. Turning, they saw why Duranos was so happy.

Four men had Winchesters leveled at them. They were trapped.

9

Captured

When the sky darkened and it began to rain Rafe led Amy along a tunnel to an opening two hundred yards from the mine's main entrance. He was taking a calculated chance that none of the outlaws had reconnoitered the area. If they missed this opening he and Amy had a chance to circle around and rejoin Ethan.

They left the mine and were scrambling across a ridge of boulders when Amy cried out. He heard the clip-clop of hoofs against stone.

Five riders had spurred their horses forward and surrounded them. Rafe's heart sank. He was outgunned and they'd easily kill him if he flinched.

The beady eyes of Carlos Duranos appraised him. Duranos dismounted and moved noiselessly toward Rafe. He moved quickly, the gun already in his hand, and struck Rafe on the head with the gunbutt. Rafe struggled to his feet and Duranos kicked him hard. The big Mexican was smiling, rain dripping from the brim of his sombrero. He said something guttural that sounded like a curse but Rafe was clenching his arm in pain and never heard the words. Duranos kicked him in the ribs and the shock sent Rafe backward, darkness spinning before his eyes.

Amy's hands were tied behind her back and she was lifted into a saddle. She watched Duranos kick Rafe. He turned to her and said, 'You will have the pleasure of watching him die later,' and his eyes were small and dirty like the markings on a potato.

Rafe was attempting to rise, blood dripping from the gash on his head. He was holding his ribs. Duranos holstered his pistol and struck Rafe with his fist. Rafe went down, unconscious. Duranos took Rafe's gun and slipped it behind his belt. They tied Rafe's hands and strung a rope from his belt to the saddle pommel.

'Help me get him to his feet, Davis.'

Davis, fat as a bull and just as smelly, came over and they lifted Rafe to his feet. Rafe was mumbling and opened his eyes. They let him stand there in the rain until he came to his senses.

'We've got a surprise for you at camp,' Carlos said with a wet smile. 'Dutch is gonna be real happy to see you.'

Duranos and Davis mounted their horses. Davis rode with Amy, forcing her on to the horse's rump as he climbed into the saddle. Duranos saw Davis squeeze Amy's breast. Then Davis turned away from her and flicked the reins.

'You best not bruise her, *amigo*,' Duranos warned. 'Dutch, he wants her all to himself.'

Davis laughed. His fat, pock-marked face wrinkled like a worn cloth and when he laughed. 'A little touch didn't hurt her none. A ripe woman like this is good to touch.'

They rode in silence, Davis leading. Amy had to lean forward on to Davis to keep from falling off. She kept her eyes shut and didn't speak. Duranos rode with Rafe following on the rope, stumbling along like a leashed dog trying to keep pace.

After a while Duranos looked back at his prisoner. 'One of the men said he saw you before, in San Antonio at a cantina. He said you were good with a gun.'

Rafe looked at Duranos without speaking.

'You are ashamed, maybe, because I took you so easily.' Duranos laughed. 'I think maybe you wish you had a gun now, huh? But the gun did you no good, *amigo, madre dios*! I can take you without a gun!' When he laughed Amy opened her eyes and turned her head. Rafe saw her look directly at him. Again, she had that look of defiance even as a prisoner with her hands tied.

Rafe's gaze moved from Amy to Duranos. Loud enough so Amy could hear Rafe said, 'This isn't over yet.'

Duranos tossed his head back and laughed again. 'So what will you do? I think you will die poorly. A man like you who is taken so easily, you will beg for your life before Dutch kills you.'

The sky was like a wall of black granite as they made their way down the hill. Occasionally, Duranos would look back at Rafe and laugh as if he was looking at the funniest sight in the world.

It was still raining when they reached the mine. Lightning flickered in the lavender night like the flames of oil lamps being snuffed out by the wind. When they passed the assay shack Rafe saw smoke whipping from the smokestack and there was a fire just inside the mine entrance. He made a mental note of the distance between the mine entrance and the shack. They were taken to the mine where Ethan, Ben, Bobby, and Adam were held prisoner by four men with rifles. Each of them had his hands tied behind his back and was sitting propped against the mine wall. Rafe felt a wave of fear and disappointment sweep over him at the sight of his friends.

Duranos pulled Amy from the saddle and told her to sit near the fire. 'I want you nice and warm for Dutch,' he said. Rafe was pushed in the direction of Ethan. Duranos was grinning.

'Sit here, *amigo*, and think how much you wish you had a gun. Sit here with your friends and have a pleasant visit.'

Still chuckling, Duranos went from the mine.

Rafe looked over the four guards. Killers by the look of them; hard, vicious men who killed without a conscience. He turned to Ethan. 'You got a plan yet?'

'Ask them to surrender.'

There was nothing else to say so they sat quietly in the mine listening to the rain fall. Amy sat near the fire, staring blankly into the flames. An hour later Duranos returned with Gault. Gault came over and slugged Rafe in the mouth. Rafe sprung to his feet and tried to head-butt the rancher but it was useless with his hands tied behind his back. Gault kicked him in the groin and Rafe went down again.

Rafe said, 'You're a brave man against someone with his hands tied.'

'I'm not trying to prove anything to you,' Gault said. 'I just don't like you.'

They all stood up and the four men stood that way a moment watching the outlaws.

'This is a pretty sight,' Duranos said.

They heard Amy gasp and Dutch Williams walked in from the rain.

He took off his Stetson and shook rainwater from the brim. He looked at Amy and a greasy smile spread across his blistered face. Rafe was shocked by his appearance. The fire had burned a swath through his hair, blistering his skin which had mottled and become brown. A few tufts of hair still clung to his scalp, but most of his head was a mass of dead, peeling skin. There were festering sores on his face, particularly near his eyes. The eyebrows were gone and he studied the prisoners with dark pupils, blinking slowly and watching them with the emotionless appraisal of a lizard. His upper lip had burned and now it was like a thin purple scar above his yellow teeth.

'You find my appearance shocking?' he asked. 'I can see you are disgusted by this' — his hand gestured to the dark blisters near his eyes — 'but these are only superficial.'

Dutch walked up to Rafe and gently caressed his face with a scarred hand. 'Your skin is still so perfect, so smooth, like the girl's skin. Should I begin with her or save her for last?'

'Go to hell,' Rafe managed to rasp. He tried to recoil from the outlaw's touch but he was bound too tightly.

Dutch put his face close to Rafe. 'Undoubtedly I will, and won't it be nice if you joined me.' Dutch spun on his heels, spurs jangling, and walked over to Amy. Taking a fistful of hair, he pulled her to her feet. He unbuttoned her shirt and placed his hand inside, groping for a breast. 'Soft.'

Together the four prisoners lurched forward to stop him but then Duranos and Gault had their guns out. The other outlaws lifted their rifles. Dutch looked at them over his shoulder.

'You're all so loyal to each other even in defeat. How charming.'

Dutch turned his attention again to Rafe. Gault pushed Rafe toward Dutch who had picked up the broken handle of a shovel. Dutch swung the handle in a wide arc and before Rafe could react the handle cracked against his ribs and a thousand pinpoints of pain racked his body. He doubled over and Dutch hit him again, this time on the back of his legs. He sprawled on the ground, breathing heavily through clenched teeth.

'I'm going to reward you for your loyalty to your friends a little bit at a time,' Dutch said, looking at the other prisoners. 'A fine group of friends you all are. And you worked so hard to save the girl. How noble. I think some of you should be rewarded with a quick death.'

He reached out and pulled Bobby Shepard by the shirt until they were standing together near the fire.

Bobby nervously licked his lips. 'You can't get away with this,' he said defiantly, 'If you surrender now Ethan will see to it you get a fair trial, and I know a jury looks favorably on outlaws that see the light and return stolen money.'

Duranos laughed and Gault made a derisive snort through his nostrils.

Dutch took his gun from its holster and held it to Bobby's chest. Dutch shook his head wistfully and said, 'So young and so stupid,' before pulling the trigger. The explosion reverberated loudly in the cavern and Amy flinched, holding her hands to her head. The bullet tore a hole through Bobby's chest and exited through his back. He fell straight to the floor without making a sound, a dark fountain of blood pumping through the gaping hole between his shoulder blades. He fell to his knees and flopped forward on his face, his body twitching and convulsing.

Amy screamed.

Rafe strained against the rope but it was wound tighter than a bowstring. Bobby's body twitched for some time as a pool of blood spread out around him. Rafe felt his breath coming in short gulps and his mouth was terribly dry. He tried to get saliva going with his tongue but it was no use. There was a ringing in his ears and a long while passed before he realized it was the memory of the gunshot, trapped in his mind like an echo that never fades.

Dutch leaned over and slapped Amy. She immediately stopped screaming and curled up in a ball, covering her head with her arms. She sat there making small sobbing noises as the rain poured down.

'We don't need any more of that, now

do we?' Dutch said. When he smiled it gave him the appearance of a grinning skull, the light from the campfire throwing shadows at his face. He was looking at Rafe.

'Now you must be feeling poorly. I suppose feeling bad is something you're not accustomed to, am I right?'

Rafe didn't respond.

'You understand my face hurts? You understand what you did to me? I'll have to pay the whores in San Antonio extra to be with me. They won't like it so much to be with someone that looks like me.'

'You'll pay in hell, you madman!' Ethan had pulled himself up and strained against his bonds. Dutch went over to Ethan and whipped his head with the butt of his gun. Ethan slumped back, a whipsaw of blood on his forehead.

Dutch turned to Gault and Duranos and said, 'Check on the men. There's still those goddamn Indians out there and I don't want any more surprises.'

Gault looked at Bobby's body before leaving with Duranos. Rafe watched him and saw the fear in his face. This was something he hadn't planned on. Now he was involved in a murder and it was eating away at him. Rafe almost felt sorry for him. But having Gault realize his mistake at this point was a hollow victory.

Dutch turned his attention again to Amy. 'My little bird.' He waved his hands like a bird and smiled wickedly, prancing in a circle around Amy, stomping his boots in the dirt so his spurs jingled. 'A sweet little bird so far from home.'

Amy brought her head up in astonishment at the sight of this madman dancing in the dirt.

He moved closer and the fear grew in her. She felt her pulse beating in her throat as he hooked his arms under hers and forced her up. His wretched face was close to hers, his fetid breath overpowering her. His eyes looked down into her soul and his scarred lips were creased in a horrifying smile. A tear formed in her eye and rolled down her cheek.

'So pretty,' he said, licking the tear from her face. When his tongue touched her skin she recoiled in disgust. She twisted in his arms, trying to force herself backward with all her strength. Jerking her right arm free she slashed a hand across Dutch's mouth, doing her damnedest to rip at him with her nails.

Dutch let her go and laughed. A deep, throaty laugh that echoed throughout the mine. His men were watching him closely now, nervous themselves because of his erratic behavior.

'You think a little pain will stop me?' Dutch looked around at his captives. He looked at Bobby Shepard's body, brought his boot back and kicked the corpse. All four men struggled against their bonds in anger and Dutch laughed at their futile efforts. Then he dragged Amy away from the fire and tied her with the others. All five were then shackled together with ropes and chains.

One of Dutch's men, Ellroy, said, 'What about the body?'

'Leave it. I want them to see nothing else.'

'But it'll stink before long.'

'Leave it!' Dutch barked.

Dutch appraised his captives once more.

'Sweet dreams.'

Smiling, he went from the mine just as a flash of lightning split the night, followed by a crash of rolling thunder.

10

Old Bear

Black Wolf moved like a shadow among the dripping trees and looked about. The rain made the air cold and the earth smelled of dampness and decay. His breath made small clouds and he was reminded that if he remained alive the lawman would give him a new horse and blankets. That was something to look forward to as he peered into the darkness watching for any sign of Old Bear.

He passed beyond the mine where his white friends were held captive. One of them had died and he thought it was the young boy. Black Wolf didn't feel any sense of regret at the knowledge of Bobby Shepard's death, but a sense of purpose guided his movements as he planned a way to free the others. Death was something that happened and there was no way to hide from it.

He found a sign of Old Bear. Yes, it was his spoor, not a day old, the trail leading to a place below the tree line where the berries were ripening in the bush.

He stood upon a low outcropping of rock. Old Bear had gone this way, lumbering slowly, wary as always. Black Wolf took pleasure in remembering the day he found the grizzly cub. He had been young then too, and he recalled what these mountains and valleys were like before too many white men came to wage war on all the tribes. In those days before the whites were many, Black Wolf hunted in these hills with his father. One day they found the dead grizzly bear, murdered by a foolish white man who killed the bear in fear. Only a white man killed in fear without thinking.

They heard the cub's plaintive cries and retrieved him from a thicket where it cowered in fear, shivering from cold and hunger. The cub was cut along the ribs but the knife hadn't penetrated far. The little bear must have escaped its attacker and hidden among the brambles.

Black Wolf kept the bear in his wickiup until it was healed and then returned it to the hills were it made its own way. Black Wolf had bonded with the small grizzly, although he never thought of it in those terms. For Black Wolf, the grizzly was a natural part of his environment and as the years progressed he marked the bear's growth and watched him often as he fished in the many streams and rivulets. The bear knew him as he knew the bear, and they grew to manhood together in the years before the white eyes came.

I am coming to visit you Old Bear, he thought, and together we will make dark medicine for the burned man.

He gave little thought to the rain and cold as he followed a trail through a small canyon until the path widened into a grove of trees. Not far now. Old

Bear might be resting.

Lightning danced like the shafts of splintered arrows in the sky. The minutes passed like black tides as he strode along, remembering this path from many years, making his way by memory and confidence. The foolish white eyes stumbled through the dark because they tried to watch their footing but Black Wolf made his way through the wilderness by instinct.

The irony of the situation was not lost on him. Black Wolf accepted long ago the ways of the world and lived in that world a content man. The white man had taken the land of his fathers and brothers and would take more long after he was gone. Now Black Wolf would save the lives of some white men and kill others.

His eyes darting over the terrain, he reined his horse and listened. A shifting of weight in the dark underbrush, barely perceptible, told him Old Bear's location. The rain had diminished to a drizzle and he found a fresh pawprint filling slowly with rain. His mind was clear and he tried to remember the old songs and some of the chants he remembered easily:

> *I will dance in the dark rain and*
> *prepare for battle!*
> *I will dance in the forest of my*
> *father!*
> *I will sing the evil-slaying prayer*
> *under the law of lightning!*

He crossed a stream and followed the bear prints along the bank. He had not gone far when he saw Old Bear move away from the bank and disappear behind some trees. Black Wolf dismounted and waited. He could wait a long time and not be disturbed because Old Bear would return when he was ready. There was only the sound of rain dripping on to leaves and falling gently across the stream, and then the sound of the stream softly gurgling over a twisted gorge of rock. After a time the grizzly emerged from the underbrush and plodded toward Black Wolf who never moved as the bear inspected him. The grizzly's nostrils flared and he snorted, raising himself on his hind legs. A deep growl came from the bear before he lowered himself and circled Black Wolf and his horse. The horse flicked its tail out of nervousness but otherwise never moved. The grizzly completed the circle and moved off into the brush again.

Black Wolf mounted his horse. It is a good thing to have friends other than man, he thought, now the death of evil men will happen in the holy land of his fathers: *Aya-na-ta-ya!* The trail of the burned man will cross the trail of Old Bear! Now is the time of cutting throats when the blood of the evil men will feed the earth! *Ya-ta-eh-ni-ya!* Black Wolf made a clicking sound and snapped the reins gently, urging his horse along the shallow stream.

I will sing a blessing for the spirit of the bear!

185

*I will dance for the hunter's
  boldness!
Black God be with me in this
  pursuit!*

Black Wolf rode along with the
stream, smelling the cool rain-swept air
and recalling his youth when he rode
with his father in these hills, and for a
moment he felt free. He wasn't thinking
any longer of the struggle he faced but
of happier times.

The rain had almost stopped. It was
almost morning and there was still
time. The air was crisp. Abruptly, the
trees were larger along the stream and
the mountain was closer, a mass of
obsidian beneath a wall of rainclouds.
Black Wolf looked back once, satisfied
the bear was following him.

He rode up the stream for two hours
and when the water deepened he took
the horse up on the bank. There were
no antelope or deer because the scent
of the bear followed him closely. But
there were squirrels and birds yattering

in the foliage. Twice he saw raccoons peering at him from an overhang of dripping leafery. Little bandits, he thought, waiting for Old Bear to pass.

Once some squirrels chattered angrily from the trees and surprised his horse, which bucked under him. The horse threw back its head and neighed. Black Wolf clicked his tongue and patted the horse's mane.

He thought about the lawman as he rode, taking great amusement in recalling the time when Ethan had chased some bad men into these hills. The two bandits were sleeping peacefully when Black Wolf crept into their camp and stole their boots. Then he took their horses quietly away and picketed them in a hidden grove. At sunup the two bandits were besides themselves with anger and fear. They put on a good show scrambling about camp in search of their boots and horses as Black Wolf watched from a secluded thicket not sixty feet away. Without their boots or horses, the two badmen were easy to apprehend.

The first time he saw Ethan was after the war, when the white men tried to destroy each other and the old chiefs made war chants to praise the white men in their efforts to kill each other. Ethan wore the blue of a soldier and Black Wolf remembered the way the brass buttons gleamed in the sun. Ethan had a ranch with a woman and sometimes Black Wolf, who had a woman of his own at the time, would steal the cattle for food and clothing. One morning Ethan surprised him in the cattle pen. Black Wolf was intent on loosening the gate latch when he heard the hammer drawn back on a gun. That was very surprising because Black Wolf never heard Ethan coming. 'You walk quietly like an Indian,' Black Wolf had said. The future lawman was smiling, and then he surprised Black Wolf again by placing his gun carefully in the holster, but never taking his eyes from Black Wolf.

'Where did you learn English?' Ethan had asked him.

'A preacher who sang the praise of your God Jesus taught me.'

Ethan appraised him for a moment. 'You have a woman nearby?'

'In the hills.'

'Take what cattle you need from time to time.'

From that simple meeting Ethan forged a friendship with Black Wolf. It was easier to keep this man as a brother rather than fight him, Black Wolf conjectured.

Last night Black Wolf dreamed a gleaming elk skull spoke to him of the old days when his family were a proud people and their numbers were many. He took this vision as a good omen even though he knew deep in his heart the good days of his people were over. He reveled now in the battle against the outlaws led by the burned man.

Although he missed his long dead wife, Black Wolf enjoyed his solitary life. He had the advantage of knowledge of the white man's world and benefited from this in ways he could not express in English. He walked between two worlds, and the grizzly followed him.

The wind shifted and he thought there might be a break in the weather. A little before sunrise he smelled smoke as he cleared the mouth of a pass. He was on a ridge a few miles from the mine. He drew rein and looked upon the panorama of wild forest. He saw the way down and urged his horse forward.

With Old Bear following closely behind, Black Wolf rode toward the outlaw camp.

11

Torture

It rained all night. Ethan sat hunched against the rocks without speaking. Sometimes he glanced at Bobby's body and the anguish was visible on his face.

Ellroy went through Bobby's pockets and grunted with disgust when he found them empty. He kicked Bobby's body and Ethan and Rafe flinched simultaneously. The other outlaws, Carl, Davis and Wade, kept their places on the opposite side of the fire near the entrance. None of them slept.

When the sky began to lighten Rafe remembered that Ethan's Indian was out there somewhere and wondered if the Indian had given them up for dead. Their situation was desperate now and there was little chance of their survival. But knowing a little chance existed could make all the difference. All three men would be waiting for the smallest mistake; any slip-up that might give them an advantage would be exploited.

Rafe closed his eyes and pretended to sleep. He went over everything in his mind until his despair was reduced to a numbness. He went over the lay-out of the mine and the surrounding area. Their guns had been taken out of the mine, probably to the assay shack with Dutch and Duranos. The horses had to be picketed a short distance down the trail.

He still felt helpless an hour later when Gault and Duranos returned. Rafe knew what was coming and there was nothing he could do about it. They lifted him to his feet and took him out to the assay shack. A yellow sliver of sunlight was breaking over the purple ridge when Gault pushed him through the doorway. Rafe sprawled on the plank flooring, spitting dust until they lifted him to his feet again. Dutch was standing near a pot-bellied stove drinking coffee from a tin cup. It was a small one-room shack with a stove. A fire crackled in the stove's iron belly. Dutch threw some fresh wood on to the fire and Rafe saw the flames licking eagerly at the kindling before Dutch slammed the creaking door. The room was furnished with a crudely carved table and makeshift chairs. The four of them stood quietly in the center of the shack listening to the fire crackling and the wind shaking the metal smokestack. A horse whinnied in the distance.

'Sit down and have some coffee,' Dutch said to Rafe.

Rafe didn't move. He stood quietly three feet from Dutch and held his gaze. Gault and Duranos came up on each side of him and forced him into a chair. Dutch spit into his coffee and set the cup in front of Rafe.

'Drink it.'

The coffee was steaming and Rafe had an inkling of what was coming. When it was clear he wasn't going to drink it Dutch picked up the cup and poured it over Rafe's head. The pain was sharp for a moment and then his eyes clamped shut and the room spun and he heard himself take a deep breath. After a few seconds he felt a numbness begin that he hoped would last. But he knew it wouldn't. His scalp stung and he blinked hot coffee from his eyes.

'Did you enjoy that?' Dutch asked.

Rafe had to force himself to speak over the pain. 'I'll see you in hell,' he said.

'That's very good. A man who doesn't know when he's whipped. I think we can do this for a long time and still you're a tough man, still you won't admit defeat. But after a time you'll understand my pain and we'll become like brothers of the fire.'

'You better kill me,' Rafe said, 'because you aren't going to get any satisfaction from this.'

'You have no idea what satisfies me,' Dutch gloated.

'He's still a tough guy,' Gault said fiercely.

'He has confidence,' Duranos said, 'but it always ends the same.'

Rafe took a breath and steeled himself for further pain. He wondered how much he could actually endure.

Dutch filled a tin plate with hot ashes from the stove. He nodded at Duranos and Gault. 'Hold him.' They held his arms as Dutch unbuttoned the top of Rafe's shirt and poured the ashes on to his chest.

The world spun into a red haze punctuated by pinpoints of blackness that expanded around him like a heavy black shawl; then he heard a small guttural sound and wondered who was moaning before realizing he was the one moaning. The scream was ripped from him without warning and mingled in the air with the satisfied laughter of Dutch Williams. The room was bathed in firelight and then blackness, and from the blackness the scarred, grinning visage of Dutch floated like a harbinger of death surrounded by the scent of burning flesh.

'This is good for you, huh?'

Some time passed and he heard Dutch say, 'I'm going to burn every inch of your flesh before I start on your face.'

Dutch removed the glass casing from an oil lamp and set it on the table. 'Roll up his sleeves.'

Gault and Duranos held Rafe and pushed up the shirtsleeve on his left arm.

Rafe's voice was a rasp, but his words were audible. 'I heard your mother was a cow-camp whore.'

Dutch leaned over the table and slugged him. His fist struck Rafe on the jaw and the force of the blow would have toppled him from the chair if not for Duranos holding him steady.

'He's got a lot of sass,' Gault said.

Dutch was watching Rafe like a dog waiting for food. Part of Rafe's shirt had caught fire from the ashes and he squirmed in the chair, patting his shirt with his elbows to smother the flames.

'You look like a chicken,' Duranos said. 'Don't he look like a chicken, Dutch?'

Dutch laughed. 'A little chicken with smoking wings.'

Duranos held Rafe's left hand over the open lamp. He jolted and tried to pull away but they held him fast. The pain was instantaneous. Rafe balled his fist and felt another scream rising to the surface. Then they let him go and he yanked his fist away. Rafe slumped over the table clutching his hand.

Dutch went over to a corner of the shack and hoisted a pick. The handle was broken at the base but there was enough wood left for Dutch to heft the pick easily with one hand. But Dutch went to the stove and opened the belly door. The fire was biting at the wood like a mass of hungry demons. Dutch slipped the point of the pick into the blaze.

'Give it a minute,' he said. 'We'll heat that up and see what's what.'

Gault made a guttural laugh. 'He looks nervous.'

'You feel any guilt over this?' Rafe was looking at Gault.

'It doesn't matter, and you best keep your mouth shut.'

'I think Bobby mattered. That was the mistake you made, Gault, you didn't think at all.'

'That was Dutch's doing.' Gault sucked in a lungful of air and watched the pick resting in the flames as if it would tell him something.

'Ethan's not going to forget Bobby that easily.'

'What is this?' Dutch said, 'Have you forgotten your friends are my prisoner?'

Duranos laughed. 'That's right, Dutch, he forgets like an old woman.'

A few minutes later Dutch pulled the pick from the fire. He examined the point and chortled with satisfaction when he blew on the metal and the smoldering iron glowed like a piece of the sun.

Duranos peeled off Rafe's shirt and

Dutch touched the pick to his shoulder. When the hot iron touched Rafe's flesh it sizzled and a tornado of smoke spun from his shoulder. He tried to bend away but the ropes held him to the chair and Duranos made sure he didn't tip himself over.

Dutch repeated the procedure on the opposite shoulder. The pain began immediately and in moments Rafe was sweating.

'These are small burns,' Dutch explained. 'And yet you are experiencing discomfort.'

Dutch walked around Rafe, waving the pick like a wand at various parts of his body but never touching him. 'There are so many tender places to choose from.' He let the point touch Rafe's arm and pressed the metal into his flesh as if he were branding him. Dutch made three striped brands on Rafe's left bicep. Rafe clenched his teeth, fighting the nausea. He concentrated on his clenched fist, hoping to distract himself from the pain, but he was losing the fight. He heard a horse whinny somewhere outside and not far from the shack when Dutch branded his right bicep with three matching stripes.

'That looks just like war paint on his arms,' Duranos said as he admired Dutch's handiwork, 'except it don't wash off.'

Dutch traced the point across Rafe's face below his left eye. Rafe shook his head back furiously, the sweat and spilled coffee spinning from his hair like dirty rain.

Another horse neighed in the distance and Dutch turned his head. His expression changed from glee to concern.

'Duranos, go see what that is.'

Duranos nodded, pulled his gun, and went from the shack.

Gault said, 'You think those Indians found us?'

'I hope so.'

Gault couldn't hide his astonishment. 'You have some kind of idea that having Sioux on our trail is healthy?'

'This isn't the time for you to be telling me anything.' Dutch's voice was a rasp and his eyes blazed.

'Just kill him and get this over with.' Gault was disgusted. Things had gotten out of control too quickly and the Sioux could make their situation desperate.

Dutch shrugged and turned his attention back to Rafe. 'No, we'll continue this later. Take him back to the mine.'

Gault didn't like it, but he did as he was told. He untied Rafe and let him pull his still smoldering shirt on. Then Gault pushed him through the door. Rafe looked around but there was no sign of life. The other men had to be down the trail near the horses.

Rafe saw Amy huddled against the wall as Gault shoved him into the mine, and later he would remember Amy staring at him with tears in her eyes before he sank into unconsciousness.

12

Escape

He was not unconscious long. Only a brief period passed when his mind reeled from the growing pain and he swam along a dark stream, all the time somehow still aware he was lying on the mine floor. His eyes opened and focused on Bobby's body which lay nearby. He stared at the body for some time, trying to gather his thoughts which were clouded from pain.

A feeling of anguish came over him and he forced himself to a sitting position. He could feel the line where Dutch had burned him beneath his left eye. He flinched at the pain.

Ethan and Adam were watching him but neither man said a word. Rafe knew Ethan was suffering over a guilt that he was responsible for Bobby's death. The remorse was etched on his face and Rafe never felt so sad before.

Amy was looking at him. Her expression was one of alertness and he tried to reassure her with a shrug and faint nod of his head. He didn't feel that confident but the way she continued staring at him led him to believe she was waiting for some kind of sign from him. But there was nothing he could do. All the same, Amy continued to watch him with wide eyes and then he understood as he followed the movement of her gaze. Black Wolf passed in front of the mine entrance, not ten feet from Ellroy, Davis, Carl and Wade. Their backs were to the entrance and they never saw him. Rafe had no doubt that Black Wolf was very good in a fight, but he was outnumbered.

A shadow fell across the mine entrance and Carl turned his head as the grizzly came into the mine, slashing Carl with his massive paw. The grizzly's paw tore away the right side of Carl's face as he tried to rise. In his struggle to reach his feet Carl stumbled, screaming and clutching his bloody face, and the grizzly swatted him again before clamping his jaws around Carl's head. The grizzly shook Carl back and forth like some huge demonic dog shaking a meaty bone. The sounds of Carl screaming and the grizzly growling in fury echoed through the cavern.

In that same instant Black Wolf was in the mine. He appeared before Rafe and slashed through the ropes that bound him. In seconds Black Wolf had freed all of the captives. Black Wolf had reacted so quickly that Ellroy and Wade never saw him enter the mine.

Ethan sprang forward as Wade drew his gun. He piled into Wade, knocking the gun from his hand. Adam was on Ellroy in the same instant and the two men were fighting furiously. Adam had his arms encircling Ellroy's neck. Ellroy pinned Adam's arms to his side and used his knee to pummel him in the groin. Adam sagged and Ellroy broke free, swinging on Adam with hard, fast blows. Adam covered his head with his arms as he went down.

Rafe and Amy watched in horror as the grizzly ripped the flesh from Carl's corpse. Seemingly dissatisfied that his prey was dead, the grizzly slashed at Carl time and again, rendering the upper portion of Carl's body into a mass of dripping ligaments.

Ben jumped to his feet and barreled into Davis. He locked his hand on Davis's wrist, struggling for control of the holstered Colt. 'You mangy cur!' Ben said between gritted teeth. Davis knocked Ben to the side, pulled his gun and shot the old cowhand in the chest. Ben grunted and fell back. Then Davis rushed out with Ellroy behind him.

Ethan was landing good punches on Wade. Then they were grappling again, but Ethan was in control. Wade must have known he was losing the fight. In desperation he forced Ethan to the side and both men tumbled into the fire. They rolled over and in seconds their shirts were burning. Ethan's fist rocked Wade's jaw several times and then Ethan was up quickly, brushing the hot coals from his shirt and trousers.

Ethan grabbed a shovel and swung it across Wade's legs as he leapt from the fire. There was a cracking sound as the shovel struck Wade's left leg. He was down again, pulling his gun. The shovel came down on his ribs and this time the cracking sound was loud and distinct. The grizzly stopped thrashing with Carl's body and turned its attention on the man whimpering a few feet in front of him. Wade's breathing was labored, wheezing. He glared at Ethan and attempted to point his gun at the lawman. He was too weak and the gun dipped, spun once around his finger, and fell to the ground.

Ethan said, 'Adam, you all right?'

Adam nodded, pulled himself up and limped toward Rafe. The fight happened so quickly that all Rafe and Amy could do was watch.

The grizzly moved toward Wade who

was pulling himself along the floor, his legs useless, driven by fury.

'Sumbitches,' he muttered, 'Sumbitches ain't gonna leave me die here like this . . . '

Ethan wiped the dust from his face with his sleeve and took a breath. 'I reckon I'll do just that,' he said and shoved Wade forward. Wade sprawled under the grizzly's nose. The grizzly sniffed once, pinned Wade with his paw, and tore his upper body to pieces as he had done to Carl.

Satisfied his second prey was dead, the grizzly sniffed the air, turning his impassive gaze upon Ethan before settling on Rafe. A low rumbling that he realized was a growl emanated from the huge bear as the animal rose up. They stepped back and Rafe thought it was unfair he should be killed by a bear after all he had been through when Black Wolf stepped out of the shadows and raised his hand.

They watched as the grizzly sniffed the air before slowly settling on all four legs again. He nosed at Wade's body before once again taking it in his jaws and dragging it slowly from the mine. Black Wolf turned to Ethan and said, 'Lucky for you Old Bear was hungry.'

Ethan picked up Wade's gun. He looked about the cavern and said, 'Damn!'

Ellroy was gone. In the confusion he must have slipped out.

'You have little time,' Black Wolf said without emotion. 'The Sioux will be here soon.'

Rafe and Amy went to Ben's side but it was no good. The old timer had passed, a strangely content look on his face. 'He died fighting,' Rafe said. 'That's all a man can ask for.'

Amy fought back the tears. She would mourn later. Now she knew she had to be strong. But she also knew her resistance was breaking down. They had to finish this soon.

They went to the entrance and peered out. There was no sign of life. The grizzly had dragged Wade's body off and was contentedly chewing at the eviscerated corpse.

'Here are your weapons,' Black Wolf said. He pointed to a pile of holsters and rifles. 'When I arrived three men were in the shack. Now nobody is in the shack. The Sioux chief is called Three Crows. He will kill all those he captures.'

Ethan looked at Rafe. 'They worked you over pretty bad.'

'I'll be all right, Marshal.'

'I figured you'd live. But can you function well enough to get through this?'

'I'm still in this. Don't doubt that for a moment.' But Rafe wished he felt as confident as he sounded.

Ethan squinted in the morning light. 'I reckon Dutch has beat us twice now and I don't figure on letting him do it a third time.'

Rafe and Adam strapped on their guns and picked up their rifles. Then Ethan found his gun and holster and for a moment the three men were engrossed in checking their weapons. The air was filled with the sound of Winchesters levered and the click of cartridges striking metal. With the grizzly gone, Amy walked over to Wade's body and took the holster from his corpse. Rafe saw the concern in Ethan's face.

'She's got a right now, more than the rest of us after what she's been through,' Rafe said.

Ethan nodded. Amy came over and Ethan handed her Wade's gun. 'I want a rifle, too,' she said.

The outlaws had left a shotgun in the mine and Rafe fetched it for Amy. She snapped open the chamber to make certain it was loaded and once again Rafe found himself admiring this woman's courage.

Adam looked around. 'That goddamn Injun has up and disappeared on us again.'

Rafe looked about quickly. Sure enough, Black Wolf was nowhere in sight.

'Doesn't that bother you any when he does that?' Rafe asked.

Ethan pulled a cheroot from his vest and snapped a match to life with his thumb. He inhaled slowly, enjoying the tobacco. 'It'd bother me a lot more if he wasn't around,' he said.

'That Indian has done right by us,' Rafe said.

They walked down the trail side by side as the sun broke free of the clouds and the day dawned fresh and bright. The horses were scattered and they spent an hour rounding them up. Rafe had to replace his dead horse so he picked one of the outlaws' horses, a brown roan.

Ethan followed a course that led them down the slope and soon they heard gunfire. They came in sight of a meadow a few minutes later and saw the remainder of the outlaw gang in furious battle against the Sioux. The outlaws were outnumbered, the sound of their guns echoing dully in the still morning air. Immediately Ethan halted and slipped from his saddle.

'They've had it,' he said. 'There's not enough cover.'

They watched as the outlaws scrambled for cover in a small copse of brush but the Sioux had already swung around and were picking them off.

'It's a matter of time,' Adam said. 'You see Dutch or Gault?'

Ethan tried to make out the shapes far below.

'I don't see them or the Mexican. Looks like Davis and Ellroy and a few others.'

They tethered the horses and crept closer, moving slowly and with care. They were on a small hill overlooking the meadow, about a hundred and fifty yards from the outlaws. Ethan paused and pointed to the left. Glancing across the meadow they saw more Sioux riding fast from a shallow arroyo. The outlaws were now completely surrounded.

The outlaws were taken in minutes. All were seriously wounded but the

Sioux were plainly delighted with their prisoners. The Sioux built a bonfire quickly and with the flames raging they heaved one of the more seriously injured outlaws onto the flames. As the flames licked at his clothes the outlaw tried to rise but he was too weak. A red spot spread out from his belly across his chest and Rafe thought he was gut shot. In seconds he was covered in flames and his body contorted grotesquely as the fire transformed him into a charred husk. The Sioux went wild, dancing and singing around the bonfire. When they settled down some time later they made posts from saplings and tied the other five outlaws along a makeshift fence.

'The one on the far right is Ellroy,' Adam pointed out. 'He would have been better off if that grizzly got him.'

'I don't see Dutch or Gault and that Mexican. There's nothing to do now but watch,' Ethan said without remorse.

The Sioux spent the better part of an hour killing the men. They took their scalps first and made a great show of celebrating their victory. There was continued singing and dancing mingled with the stark moans of the dying outlaws.

After the men were scalped Amy said, 'I'm not watching this,' and turned her back on the spectacle.

The Sioux had taken the dynamite from one of the outlaws' saddle-bags and the sight of the explosives sent them into another round of ecstatic celebration. They whooped and hollered, waving the slender TNT sticks in the air.

'They'd be lucky they don't blow themselves to kingdom come,' Adam said, shaking his head in disbelief.

One of the braves taunted Ellroy with the dynamite. Ellroy, barely alive, tried to spit at the brave. All of the braves were highly amused by this weak show of defiance. Then the brave forced the dynamite stick into Ellroy's mouth. Ellroy clamped his teeth and forced the stick free but he succeeded only in angering the Sioux who promptly slashed open Ellroy's belly with his knife before ramming the dynamite down his throat. Only the tip protruded and the brave pulled a flaming branch from the bonfire and lit the fuse as Ellroy's intestines slid down his legs like a nest of bloody snakes.

'Holy Christ!' Adam rasped.

The detonation tore Ellroy to pieces. They promptly devised similar tortures for the remaining men. The braves turned their attention to Davis then and he began wailing. He whimpered and moaned and cried and made hurt, gurgling sounds. The Sioux chanted in unison with his plaintive cries. Rafe was repulsed by the brutality yet unable to avert his eyes.

Something struck his shoulder and it took him a moment to recover from his surprise before he realized Amy was striking him with her fists. He winched in pain as she struck his burned arm. She stopped when she realized she had hurt him. Rafe held her wrists.

'I'm . . . I'm sorry,' she stammered, 'I

215

can't . . . it's too much. I can't watch men suffer like that.' She pulled herself closer and sobbed quietly. Rafe held her without speaking. 'They had it coming,' Rafe said at last. 'Those are the same men who wanted to rape you, the same men that tried to kill us all.'

She pulled away and wiped her eyes. 'It's not right,' she said. 'Even if they are bad men. Nobody should suffer like that.'

'They didn't give Bobby a chance,' Ethan said angrily, 'and this is playing out the way they set it up.'

'That doesn't make this right,' Amy said. 'Nothing makes torturing a man the right thing.'

'It's still justice,' Ethan said. 'You think hanging would have been easier for them? Thinking about that noose is like a torture and it goes on a sight longer than anything those braves have planned for those boys.' Ethan paused, trying to find the right words but he knew there was no way to make it sound right. 'Hanging a man's just as

216

dirty. The only difference is a judge makes it happen and the dying's just as slow. I've seen a man kick the air for most of an hour and mess himself before dying.'

Another explosion rocked the Indian camp followed by the whooping exaltation of the braves.

'It's time to find Dutch,' Ethan said.

'That crazy Injun might just be tracking them now,' Adam offered.

'I'm sure he is.'

'We bury Bobby and Ben first,' Amy said. 'We're not leaving their bodies back in that mine. We'll give them a proper burial.'

Ethan squinted, wiped his brow and adjusted his hat. He looked at Amy and then he looked down at the Sioux camp. The wailing had stopped and the outlaws were all dead now. But Dutch, Duranos and Gault were still free. They had to finish this.

'All right. Let's ride,' Ethan drawled.

★ ★ ★

They buried Bobby and Ben on a grassy hill overlooking a small lake. The three men dug a grave with the shovel and pick-axe left in the mine, taking turns clearing out the dirt from a six-foot hole under the expansive noon sky. The sunlight was a relief after the turmoil of the thunderstorm, but it made the digging more difficult. It took them the better part of two hours to dig the graves. The earth was strewn with all sizes of rocks and they used these to blanket the grave once they shoveled the dirt back in. They hoped the rocks would deter any animals from digging up the bodies.

Amy found some canvas wrapping near the mine and covered them carefully. Before tying close the shroud she placed some wildflowers in their hands, gently straightened Bobby's hair, and kissed him softly on the brow. Then she did the same for Ben. None of them spoke during the burial. Amy wept bitterly when it was all done but she didn't linger at the grave. She was strong and knew she had to stay strong. She would mourn Bobby and Ben a long time, as they all would, but over time her grief would become part of her resilience.

It was late afternoon by the time they set the last stone on the graves and Ethan wanted to place more distance between them and the Sioux.

They rode well into the night, picking their way carefully along a trail and down into the tall trees. It was a relief for them to leave the high country behind, although they knew there was still the danger from the Sioux in the area, and the unalterable fact that Dutch Williams had escaped with Gault and Duranos did nothing to cheer them.

Once again they put together a quick camp in among a strand of pine. Ethan immediately refused a campfire.

'We've had our share of luck,' he explained. 'As long as Dutch is out there we're better off keeping a mind to caution.'

Rafe settled down in the shadows with a saddle blanket to keep the chill mountain air at bay and a saddle for a pillow. He held his Colt under the blanket on his chest. Ethan was right: their luck had to run out sometime. There was no sense in taking an unnecessary risk. Amy lay down under a blanket next to him. She had not spoken since they buried their fallen friends and he had no wish to engage her in conversation now. They were all exhausted. In minutes her steady, deep breathing told him she had fallen asleep.

Rafe's body ached from his wounds; his chest had swollen and blistered quickly and he felt a continual searing pain on his arms, as if the fire had not gone away and his hand ached also. So that was something of how Dutch felt; a constant inflammation that tore at a man, peeling away his skin with his resolve.

He looked up past the silhouettes of trees and watched the stars shimmering in the firmament.

The quiver of atavistic violence that spurred them on in their mad pursuit of Dutch Williams had subsided temporarily and Rafe felt soft and pliable, almost childlike. He was tired and frightened and still hungry, although he had managed to eat some biscuits. He wanted nothing more than to sleep, but his wounds lashed at him like invisible spirits with sharp talons.

He wondered why men carried such ferocity in their hearts. As he watched the trees rippling gently in the warm night breeze he discovered he was immensely thirsty but his legs no longer responded to his will. He was caught, immobile, suffering from a scorching thirst and unable to act. The simplest of movements was impossible: he tried reaching for the canteen which seemed only yards away, and in his fevered state he watched his burned hand reaching out in front of him, clawing at air.

When he opened his eyes next Black Wolf was peering down at him, so he closed his eyes again. When he opened his eyes Black Wolf was gone. He was just tired, he told himself, and seeing things. But then Black Wolf was there, urging him to a sitting position, pulling his tattered shirt from his body.

Adam's voice came from somewhere nearby. 'I suppose if he dies the girl will be mighty upset.'

'He won't die,' Black Wolf said, 'but the pain will stay with him a long time.'

Black Wolf was gently placing a poultice on his wounds. Rafe shivered. Something sticky and cold, smelling of moss and maybe violets was applied to his burned chest. He cried out and then he saw Amy.

'Don't try to speak,' she said. 'Lie back now. You'll be all right.'

Black Wolf lashed up Rafe like a mummy, wrapping his chest with a tight cloth over the muddy adhesive. 'Leave this on until the itching becomes unbearable,' Black Wolf instructed him. 'Then bathe in warm water. About five days. But no sooner than that.'

'What is that, some kind of Injun medicine?' Adam grunted.

'It will help heal him.'

'It's also gonna make him smell a sight worse, and he ain't smellin' pretty now.'

Amy eased Rafe down and wrapped him again in the horse blanket. His eyes fluttered and she felt his body slowly relax.

'He feels so warm, as if he has a fever.'

'Keep him covered. His fever will break by morning.'

Amy pulled her blanket over, covered herself, and pressed down next to Rafe, looping her arm over his chest.

Rafe slept soundly but woke once. His fever had broken and he watched the stars as if he were seeing them for the first time. The air was crisp and clear in his lungs and a warm breeze ruffled Amy's hair. The sky was hard and dark blue but after a while the sky lightened with the sharp stars fading and he wondered when he had noticed the change. He placed his injured hand on Amy's hair, careful not to wake her, and he stroked her hair for a moment and wondered what kind of future they might have. His fatigue had been replaced by an acceptance of his limitations and the thought made him happy that he would recover. Amy was breathing lightly but regularly so he closed his eyes again and slept.

In the morning Adam and Ethan had already saddled and packed the horses when Rafe opened his eyes. Adam came out of the timber smoking a cigarette with Ethan behind. Ethan came over and looked at Rafe.

'You might live after all.'

'I'll live, but not unless I get some good strong coffee in me.'

Ethan frowned. 'I've been thinking about that myself. After we ride a couple of hours and I'm fairly certain nobody's on our backtrail, we can make a campfire. I feel out of sorts without coffee.'

Amy stirred and said something but

her voice was muffled by Rafe's shirt. He hadn't moved since he awoke, finding that he enjoyed immensely waking up with this girl in his arms. He smiled sheepishly at Ethan. Ethan didn't smile but some of the anger was gone from his eyes. They had been through a lot together in a short time.

'Hell, you got your hands full in more ways than I can count,' Ethan grunted.

'Yes, Marshal, I sure do.'

Amy stretched, yawned, looked at Rafe briefly, and smiled. When she realized Ethan was watching them she blushed furiously, gathered her blanket, and set about getting her things ready.

Black Wolf's sudden reappearance went without comment as they spent the morning following Dutch's trail. Near high noon they halted on a meadow as Black Wolf studied the tracks. 'The trail of the burned man will fork here,' the Indian said.

It wasn't long before they understood what the enigmatic Indian meant as they cleared a rise and spotted the dust from the Sioux ponies not a hundred yards from them. The Sioux were in no hurry. Two dozen of them waited in a silent row as they made their way across a sun-dappled field.

Black Wolf took the lead and Ethan noted the Sioux chief named Three Crows kept his eyes on their solitary Shoshone companion. Ethan had met Three Crows before and respected the elderly but unfriendly chief. Years later, when Ethan would read a magazine account of this day, it would be said the grizzly rode with them across the field and that Three Crows, in deference to Black Wolf and the grizzly, allowed the exhausted posse to pass unharmed; this was not true for the grizzly had already gone, but what was true was the startling fact the Sioux chief raised his hand as Black Wolf met his gaze and the defeated posse crossed the field unhindered.

Three Crows then appraised the posse and while he didn't look pleased, something that might have been respect showed in his face when he looked at them. So they passed each other on the Wind River plain, both following their own path into history.

At day's end the posse reached the top of a grade and they could see the immense forest and valley. Black Wolf pointed at the dense forest. The tall timber was dark and impenetrable. 'The burned man and two others are there,' he said. 'It is the place of spirits and only the strongest medicine man can live there.'

'What about the Sioux? Won't they go after them?' Ethan inquired.

'There is nothing to follow now but spirits.'

'What the hell does that mean?' Adam said flatly.

'Keep your guns ready. The burned man will find you soon.'

Then Black Wolf nodded to Ethan and without another word he rode away. They quickly lost sight of him as he rode into the woods.

'I'll never get used to that Injun,'

Adam grumbled. 'He speaks English but I don't understand a word he says.'

It had been a hot day and they had ridden a long while. When the sun began to sink the air cooled and they made a camp on a rise populated with old pines. Ethan allowed a small fire on the back slope and out of sight to anyone that might be watching from the valley. They enjoyed the cool air and the fresh water from a nearby creek and the smell of coffee which they drank greedily.

The nightbirds were beginning their soft chorus when they heard a high-pitched sound from far down in the valley.

Adam was up first, rifle in hand. 'What was that?'

Ethan came up next to Adam and crouched on the hilltop among a strand of trees, peering into the dark forest.

They heard it again; something like a scream only beginning and then fading quickly into an anguished wail.

Amy and Rafe came up and watched.

Nothing happened for almost ten minutes. Then a scream — and it was clearly a scream this time — rose up from the trees.

Silence.

The sound they heard next sent a chill up their spines. A wet, cackling sound echoed from the underbrush.

'What in hell is that?' Adam asked.

Rafe touched Amy's hand and he felt her shiver, but not from his touch. She knew what it was as well. He looked at the others.

'That's Dutch Williams,' he said. 'It sounds like he's laughing.'

13

Bad Omens

Down in the darkness there were voices.

Someone was whispering.

Hoot of owl and coyote call.

A flapping of wings. Something was moving and John Gault knew it was coming closer. Dutch Williams sat hunched across from the campfire, the flames mirrored in his feral eyes like the blazes of hell. The blisters and scars on his face pulsed with life. Duranos sat nearby, an impassive shadow among shadows.

'What is it that you fear?' he asked Gault. 'You afraid of the dark and need your mommy?' Dutch laughed, a dry, hoarse laugh before coughing up a wad of spit. He hacked the mucus loose in his throat and spit the gob at the fire where it sizzled on the log like bacon fat.

'This ain't right, us staying down here with all these dead Injuns,' Gault said sharply.

Dutch observed Gault with true astonishment. 'Once they're dead they can't hurt you.' Dutch pulled a knife from its belt sheath and traced a finger along the edge. The blade punctured his skin, although only slightly. He examined the dot of blood on his finger with the same curiosity he had shown when he looked at Gault. He jammed his bloody finger in his mouth and sucked on it eagerly. 'It's when they're alive that they can hurt you.'

Dutch stood up and looked around the ring of trees. They were camped in an Indian burial ground and the dozen platforms in the trees with their silent, shrouded occupants made Gault uneasy. That, and the noises. The darkness was alive with scurrying sounds. Something that sounded like moccasin footfalls on the leafy forest carpet.

Duranos was watching Gault, too, but in place of curiosity there was only a stoney, impassive stare. He was with Dutch because he had nothing else, and together they had the money, and no matter if money was a useless thing among the shadows of the dead.

Dutch climbed up on to the nearest platform and yanked the corpse free with quick slashes of his knife. He pulled the body down by the ankle; a stiff, brittle doll swathed in moldering blankets.

'God damn it! You got no call to do that!' Gault said harshly.

Dutch laughed again. 'God has damned us all, my friend.'

He began cutting the blanket loose from the corpse. The decaying fabric unraveled like the strands on a mummy. In a moment he had revealed the head of a woman. She had been dead a long time. Her brown skin was sunken around her skull, her mouth open in her last frozen breath. When Dutch pulled the last piece of fabric loose revealing the Indian woman's face the wind picked up and moaned among the trees. Little purling cries issued from the darkness on the camp perimeter.

'Ain't she pretty?' Dutch said. He stroked her long matted hair as if she were a thing of beauty.

'For the love of God, Dutch, stop this madness!' Gault's harsh voice rose sharply and Dutch looked at him with renewed interest. Then the anger took hold of Dutch and in that instant Gault knew their fate and the despair rose in him like a tide blotting out all other emotion.

Dutch smiled, somewhat grimly. 'Love, God, and my name all in one breath,' he said as his hands closed around the corpse's neck and his hips rocked in unison to his mad desires. The flesh and bone crushed under his powerful grip and the head broke free from the body, trailing dust.

With the decaying skull in hand, Dutch turned quickly and leaped on to Gault before he had time to react.

Gault grunted with pain as the outlaw's weight came down. The skull was obliterated into a thousand crumbling pieces. All that remained was the mesh of hair still clinging to a thin membrane of skin and clinging to Gault's face like an unholy web.

Gault whimpered in terror. He flailed his arms, gasping and choking on corpse dust, clawing desperately at the hair covering his face.

'If you need to fear something,' he heard Dutch saying as he freed himself of the hair, 'fear me! I'm alive and a man that lives and breathes and walks is to be feared, by God! Tomorrow we ride out and take what's ours! If I hear any more from you I'll leave you here to rot with these dead Indians!'

Dutch was crouched over Gault breathing into his face like a jackal before his prey. His sour breath made the bile rise in Gault's throat.

'What more do you want now that you have the money?' Gault managed to rasp.

'Vengeance!' The word snapped like a rifle shot.

'We'll take the girl again. They couldn't have gotten far. We'll ride after them and take her as hostage. This time we keep her.'

'And what if we don't find them? What if they get back to town?'

'Then we wait. Another day will come.'

Dutch stepped back, his face and body suddenly relaxing, as if the flood that welled up in his soul had quickly abated. Duranos had not moved. He seemed only mildly interested in their antics, but now he spoke.

'*Amigo*, when you are finished playing I think maybe we should look around.'

'What is it?' Dutch inquired with mild interest.

Duranos pulled up his six-gun and checked the cylinder. 'One voice can sound like an owl or a coyote.'

'This is holy ground for Indians,' Dutch said. 'They wouldn't come here at night.'

'All the same, we need to be careful. Those Sioux are still prowling and they won't take kindly to our being here.'

'He's right!' Gault said hotly, 'This is their land! If they learn what you've done to their dead they'll hunt you! They'll hunt all of us! It ain't right. You saw what they did to the others.'

Dutch considered this for a moment and when he spoke his eyes were pierced by a flickering light. 'My little babies are scared tonight.'

Dutch lit a torch and they spent an hour scouting the area on foot but found nothing. Gault was unnerved and kept his gun cocked. Once when an animal went scratching up a tree he spun and almost fired. This made Dutch roar with laughter. They searched near the bodies strung up in the trees and sometimes Dutch examined the artifacts left to aid the dead in their journey to the happy hunting ground. There were knives and bows and arrows, spears and pottery. Dutch swept it aside carelessly. Gault trembled, speaking softly to Duranos,

'He's mad, I tell you! This is the same as a sacrilege!' But Duranos was impassive, in his own silent way as uncaring as Dutch Williams.

Presently they returned to the campfire and settled in for the night but Gault couldn't sleep. His mind wavered between despair and the faint hope he might overcome his folly and retain his life. But how? John Gault was a hunted man now, an outlaw of the same ilk as this madman who snored so contentedly as the darkness closed in around them.

At first the idea of helping Dutch and his gang rob the bank had seemed foolproof. The money would get him off that infernal ranch and he could have some things for himself. Everything had gone wrong the moment Rafe Morgan rode into town. Dutch wanted his vengeance and still refused to give up the trail. So all was lost. Gault had lost everything. The money they had stolen was meaningless.

From off in the darkness came

movement. Shapes blacker than the night scuffled like unholy specters. This was the fate of the hunted, he thought bitterly. The uncertainty that comes with pursuit, an uneasiness that forced him constantly to turn his head in anticipation of capture. This was a place of bad omens.

He resolved to end it then. He reached a point where he could no longer accept the dark, unseen forces that clamored after him from the Stygian darkness. The only way to make things right was to go back and face the lawman, kill him if possible. Tomorrow he resolved to kill them all and ride as far away from Dutch Williams as possible.

But John Gault didn't like his prospects at all.

14

Gunfight!

Ethan had insisted they split into two groups and circle the outlaws. Adam said 'We did that already and got caught.'

Ethan cast him an unhappy glance. 'We do it again. This time let's try not to get caught.'

Rafe had a sense that Black Wolf was observing too as they watched the three outlaws ride a trail that curved between two granite cliffs. Ethan and Amy were circling from the opposite direction. Adam and Rafe were hunched on an outcropping, rifles ready.

Rafe and Adam went into the rocks and immediately began angling upward. A chasm separated them from Amy's position on the rocks. Now and then Rafe stopped to explore the area for

239

better leverage to keep himself from slipping. Sometimes it was difficult to keep his balance while holding the rifle, but Rafe was stubborn as the rest of them. Bracing themselves, they slogged over an incline and mounted a boulder near a scarred outcropping.

Rafe was dismayed to see that Ethan and Amy were now separated. Amy was on a ledge less than a half mile away, her red hair shining and waving in the soft wind. She carried the shotgun. She was scouting the high rocks, looking for a sign of the outlaws.

Another figure, a man with a black sombrero, was moving after her on the left.

Carlos Duranos.

It was obvious Amy was aware of his presence. She was attempting to climb a rocky area and looked over her shoulder frequently. Duranos was in no hurry. He moved slowly but with assurance, picking his way across the ledge. There was too much distance separating them. Rafe was a good shot

240

but at this distance and at such an awkward angle he knew he would never hit Duranos. He would have to shoot up but twisted to his far left in order to get the Mexican in his sights. There was no way to brace himself and the gravel under him could cause him to slip at any time. And a shot now would alert the outlaw to his presence.

Push uphill. Hope that Amy somehow saw him coming. All she needed to do was turn slightly to her right and look downhill. She would see him plain as day.

Rafe made twenty feet. Then he made another twenty feet when he realized it wasn't working. Duranos had closed the distance.

'They're too far,' Adam said. 'We can't make it in time.'

Amy was part way up the boulder but had reached an impasse. She was searching the area for better footing. Rafe and Adam were nearly parallel with them now but he still wasn't sure of his footing. There was no time. They had to take Duranos down.

Rafe decided to take the initiative and desperately half-ran, half crawled another ten yards. Setting his feet flat he stood straight as he dared while the wind picked up and he cursed softly under his breath. Invisible fingers tugged at him and he slipped. He went down on one knee hard. A jolt of pain flashed through his bone. Heaving to his feet, Rafe raised the rifle. Duranos was closer to Amy, a few feet away. He had his gun out. Amy had stopped. She was motionless on the rock. Duranos was talking to her. The wind carried the echo of their voices but they couldn't make out the words.

In one frozen instant, as Amy and Duranos faced each other, Rafe aimed and fired. The rifled boomed once but the shot missed. Rafe saw the puff of rock splinter next to Duranos in the same instant the rifle's report was carried away by the wind.

Amy saw Rafe and Adam, and at the sight of them she turned and resumed climbing with renewed vigor. Now at least she knew she wasn't alone.

Duranos turned and looked at his pursuers. He smiled. In another moment Rafe knew why Duranos was smiling. When he heard the jingle of spurs he knew Dutch Williams was behind him, playing out his part in this deadly tableau unfolding on the rocks. Adam was spinning then, swinging the rifle around and firing as the loose surface gave way and sent him sliding. Dutch shot him once and the bullet ripped through the fleshy part of his hip. By then he was falling. He went down fast, bullets chipping stone splinters and dust in his eyes as Dutch unloaded his gun.

Adam was sent tumbling. When he came to a stop he was blinded from dust and pain. Rubbing the grit from his eyes he examined his surroundings. He had fallen out of view from Dutch and Duranos but if they came searching he would be easy enough to find. The rifle was gone, dropped when he fell. He pulled himself up and forced himself back into the underbrush. He wanted to get below the tree line. When he was hidden among the trees he covered his wound with a bandanna. Rafe was nowhere to be seen. When Adam tried to move a jolt of pain flashed through him. He realized with a moan that his leg had broken in the fall.

* * *

Black Wolf appeared again just as Ethan was having a difficult time climbing up the trail. 'Getting old,' Black Wolf said.

'You and Adam like to point out my deficiencies,' Ethan grumbled.

'Means we like you,' Black Wolf said.

They were making their way slowly through a tangle of deadfall when they heard the boom of a rifle. They scrambled over a dry creek bed and up the trail until they emerged on a rise overlooking an area of rocks.

They had to be close to whatever was happening. The rifle blast had been nearby, somewhere down on those rocks. They went over a deadfall log and out of the grassy trail on to the rocks. Black Wolf lead the way past some scrub pines growing out of cracks there. He hadn't gone thirty feet when he was hit by a rifle bullet in the side. Ethan saw his tunic jump from the impact before he heard the explosion. Black Wolf took a step back involuntarily as the bullet splattered out of his lower back. He spun on his heels, reaching for his side, and sat down. Ethan hooked his arms under Black Wolf's shoulders and dragged him back behind the scrub pines for cover.

Black Wolf had a perplexed expression on his face as he examined the bullet hole in his right side. 'A very good shot for a white man,' he said.

Later on, Ethan would think that was a very funny thing for Black Wolf to say but now he was busy trying to stop the bleeding.

'The bullet went clean through. If we can stop the bleeding you might live.' Ethan cut a swath from Black Wolf's shirt and was attempting to press it on to the wound when Black Wolf pushed his arm away.

'If I let you help me I'll die in an hour. White men make poor medicine. Take me down near those trees.'

'You're as stubborn as Adam,' Ethan told him. Lifting him from his left side, Ethan half carried Black Wolf down to the trees and followed his instructions in getting a compress of mud and moss to place on the wound. When he was finished he said, 'I'll come back later and we'll get you to a doctor.'

Black Wolf smiled. Ethan was surprised. He had never seen him smile before. 'If the two of us survive this battle I would like a new coat. The mountains are cold most of the year.'

Ethan pulled a cheroot from his vest and gave it to Black Wolf. 'You drive a hard bargain,' he said. 'I imagine you'll survive and I'll have to buy you a new coat, which I can't rightly afford.' He snapped a match to life on his jeans and lit the cheroot. Ethan looked down at

Black Wolf. There was nothing more to do here. Neither man was prone to voicing sentiment, and lingering here would only jeopardize them further. Black Wolf was propped against a pine smoking when Ethan went back up the trail.

He chanced a quicker pace, no longer bothering with stealth. They knew he was here and they were waiting for him. From a position just behind the tree line he examined the rocky foothills. There was no sign of life. They had to be down on his right, hidden in those trees and scrub. Whoever shot Black Wolf had to have done so from a grouping of high boulders on the perimeter of the forest.

Ethan decided on a course that would take him down along to the right. It wasn't a choice he preferred but he couldn't see an alternative. Crossing the boulders would expose him foolishly and keeping to the perimeter offered cover. But he would be moving directly into an area where

Dutch and Duranos were in all likelihood waiting for him.

He kept about twenty feet back from the rocks, following a meandering natural trail formed by runoff from the rain. He maintained his gaze on the surrounding forest, alert for sounds or movement. Several times he encountered snarls of tree roots that forced him to circle farther out to his right than he wished.

It took him fifteen minutes to make his way down to the largest visible boulder. He was certain this was the place from which someone had shot Black Wolf. He veered away from the boulder at this point, still keeping his distance behind the tree line.

When he moved away from his position, creeping closer to the perimeter where he could look out over the boulders, he saw a glimmer on the ground. He made his way to the spot and found it immediately. A brass cartridge. Someone had fired from this position, either Dutch or Duranos.

There had been enough surprises and enough risks taken, Ethan thought, now was the time to finish this.

A quick look around the area told him nothing more. He eased forward, closer to the openness of the rocks, allowing himself to become more visible. His hope was that his movement would catch their attention and draw their fire. He timed his movements carefully in order to keep himself obstructed by the trees. He wanted them to spot him without giving them a clean shot. He was sweating now and his stomach was a bundle of knots. He wondered where Adam and Rafe were.

A pebble dropped on to a boulder twenty feet from him and rolled down into a gully. Ethan turned in the direction of the sound in the same instant he knew someone had tossed a pebble to distract him. His nerves were so tightly wound that he couldn't prevent himself from turning, so he let his body spin while throwing himself down and turning up with his gun firing. The move saved his life but one of the bullets clipped his right arm, tearing through muscle. His gun went clattering off on the rocks.

Then John Gault walked out from behind a boulder, his gun leveled at Ethan's belly. Gault was grinning. Ethan had nowhere to run.

'You had a chance, Marshal, but it's over,' Gault hissed.

'You'll never get away with it.'

'And you'll never know if I do or not,' Gault responded. 'Is that Indian dead? I had a good shot at him, didn't I?'

Ethan didn't answer. The marshal's left hand was clamped tightly to his right forearm and there was blood oozing up between his fingers.

'A nasty wound,' Gault said. 'I'm sure you'd like to have that cleaned and bandaged — however, I'm afraid one bullet hole isn't all they'll find in your body.'

Ethan saw it coming and was diving for the underbrush on his left as Gault brought up the Colt and fired. The blast tore through part of his thigh. Then he was down and rolling, desperately scrambling for cover. Up on his feet and running, without thinking, just trying to stay alive now, somehow regroup. A spur jingled. A boot struck stone. Gault was behind him, coming up fast. Ethan was following a path down into a crevice between two boulders when another shot clipped the rocks near his head.

He paused, reached into his vest and brought out the derringer. This he had learned in the war — always have a back-up gun. It was a two-shot derringer but he wouldn't get but one shot.

The sun had vaulted over the mountains, casting long shadows as the afternoon waned. Ethan, crouched near a small tree, saw Gault's shadow slinking up the trail. He jumped up, extended his arm and simultaneously cocked the derringer. Gault saw him, opened his mouth as if to say something, and Ethan pulled the trigger.

The gun bucked and spat hot lead. The bullet took Gault in the chest. A red stain bloomed on his shirt as he stumbled, his knees buckling. He plopped face first on to the rocks, his last breath gurgling in his throat.

Then Ethan lost his balance and went sliding. He was on a rocky ledge thirty feet above a chaparral thick with underbrush and small trees. A wave of disappointment swept over Ethan as he realized there was nothing for him to hold on to, and then he fell in a swirl of dust and pebbles.

★ ★ ★

Rafe was running, his senses primed, intent on closing the final distance. Raising the rifle as he ran, he levered off two shots in swift succession. He was aiming at Duranos and cursed when both shots missed. It was a foolish gamble; the distance was too great and he was off balance firing at a run. Duranos and Dutch separated when they saw him. Dutch had piled into Amy, taken her shotgun, stripped off her holster, and knocked her senseless. Now Dutch had a fistful of Amy's hair and pulled her with him into the underbrush. Rafe saw Amy break free, kick Dutch solidly in the leg before sprinting down the trail. That girl had brass!

Dutch went after Amy while Duranos held back, drawing his gun. Rafe snapped another shot with the rifle and bore down on the bandit. He was too close now for an accurate shot so Rafe hurled the rifle in an arc before Duranos could fire. Duranos ducked and braced himself against the blow. He wasn't injured but throwing the rifle had given Rafe the time he needed.

He slammed into Duranos and began pounding him with his pistol. Duranos grunted, squealed with pain as Rafe broke his nose with his gunbutt. They bucked and kicked, rolling out on to the rocks. Rafe dropped the gun but tried hitting Duranos in the face with his fist, anything to keep the pain constant and intense. Duranos squirmed fiercely and Rafe's punches slid off his chest. Duranos gouged at Rafe's eyes, forcing him back, but as he dropped away Rafe kicked him in the ribs. He heard bone crack. Duranos squealed again as he crawled for the gun. Rafe kicked him in the head and a spray of teeth and blood showered the rocks.

Duranos lashed out wildly, scraping Rafe's face. The pain had enraged Duranos and he was like a frenzied animal now, slashing blindly. Somehow he got his hands on Rafe's belt and hauled him down. Duranos drove his knee into Rafe's stomach and the air popped from his lungs. Duranos hit him but Rafe was already writhing sideways, struggling to break free while he regained his strength.

Rafe spotted the gun on the rocks and made his way toward it. Duranos scuttled along the rocks after him, diving for his feet. He managed to clutch tightly on to Rafe's trouser leg and slow him down. As soon as Rafe felt himself going down again he struck Duranos with his fist which brought another squeal from the profusely bleeding outlaw.

Rafe hit him again and again. His fist made a wet slapping sound on the outlaw's bleeding face. He balled his fist and struck so many times Rafe thought he'd broken his own hand. Duranos wouldn't let go. He clawed and whimpered and cried, eventually clamping his teeth on to Rafe's leg.

Ten feet away from the gun. Rafe dragged Duranos with him, falling and rising again as the outlaw bit into him as would a rabid dog. He stopped striking Duranos and concentrated on the gun.

Five feet. Rafe had fallen so often his knees were torn and bleeding from slamming against the rocks. He dragged Duranos the last few feet and stretched out for the gun.

His fingers closed around the grip. Rafe was flat on the boulder now, his right hand stretched out, reaching. He had it now and he looked down at Duranos who clung like a leech to his boots, still game at the end, trying to crawl his way over Rafe, the malevolence blazing in his dark eyes.

'I am going to kill you, *amigo*. I am going to choke the life from you now with my bare hands.' His breath hissed out between his broken teeth.

'Give it up. It's over.' Rafe pointed the gun at Duranos. The outlaw loosened his grip on Rafe briefly as the knowledge he had lost came into his face, but the malice was still there.

Rafe hesitated only a moment before deciding to spare the hangman a rope and pulled the trigger. The Colt roared and the bullet slammed between the outlaw's eyes and exited his skull with an eruption of blood.

Rafe looked away. He felt Duranos twitch, his body shivering in its final paroxysm. Even in death Duranos clung tightly to Rafe's leg. Rafe was forced to pry the dead man's fingers from his trousers. He loaded the gun and holstered it and found another gun and stuck it in his belt. His right hand was numb and the knuckles were bruised. He had other bruises all over his body, but the worst part were his knees. They had taken a banging on the rocks. He hobbled into the pine forest, retrieved his hat which had been knocked off when he tackled Duranos.

His swollen knees felt as if they were pierced with two hot spikes. Rafe pushed aside the pain and strained to hear. He could see down a rivulet where the copse of pines bordered a small creek. He could hear them; a splashing from downstream. He moved off the rocky plateau and went down through the pines.

He didn't have far to go. Following the stream around an outcropping of boulders, Rafe glimpsed Dutch in the trees on the right side. They had crossed the stream. Amy must be heading for the boulders on that side. Dutch was following her up onto another slab of rock.

He remembered this boulder from when he came up the trail earlier. He had gone around it because it dead-ended about sixty feet above the stream bed. Then he realized what Amy was doing. She was leading Dutch up onto the boulder knowing Rafe was behind them. Once she got up onto the slab there would be nowhere for her to run. Or for Dutch either.

Once they were up on the boulder the only thing that remained was to see who would walk down again.

He had to push on and ignore the pain that shot through his knees every time he moved. The trail wound around the boulder. He had to stoop and pull himself up between the granite slabs that towered on each side of him; and then he was up on the boulder, rising to his feet when Dutch knocked the gun from his right hand with a vicious kick. The gun clattered down the slope.

He heard Amy gasp and then he saw her up on the boulder's tip. Dutch stood between them, a six-shooter in his left hand trained on Rafe, the shotgun in his right leveled at Amy.

'All right, this is a good place for a showdown. Keep your hands where I can see them. I don't want to kill you too quickly. I rather enjoy seeing you sweat.' Dutch surveyed Rafe with his hot eyes. 'Here we are!' He gloated. 'Young lovers in the hands of an outlaw. I see you're not enjoying this. A most unfortunate situation for you both.' Dutch waved his gun at Rafe while keeping the shotgun in his right hand trained on Amy. 'I don't want to see you move. Not a muscle. Not once.'

Rafe said nothing. Dutch would have his say, and then Rafe would rush him. There was nothing else he could do.

'You have caused me a great deal of pain, my young friend, and I am truly going to enjoy watching you die.'

Dutch eyed Rafe speculatively a moment. He gestured with the shotgun barrel at Amy. 'Isn't she pretty? So sweet and lovely and frightened. I want you to think about what I'm going to do to her. In fact, I think I might let you live long enough to watch some of this.'

A fine sheen of perspiration broke out across Dutch's forehead. He licked his lips. 'But we can't have any more of this running around the countryside, now can we? No, that won't do at all.'

Dutch shot Rafe in the leg. The blast was thundering. When the six-gun barked Amy involuntarily cupped her ears with her hands and flinched. Rafe was down on one knee and Dutch shot him again. The second bullet ripped through the flesh of his right forearm.

'That should about do it,' Dutch remarked. 'I don't expect to see you holding a gun for a long time, at least if you were going to live, which I have no intention of allowing.'

Rafe was sprawled on the boulder writhing in pain. For a long moment Dutch regarded Amy with his glittering eyes. Then he moved forward and placed the muzzle of the shotgun an inch from Amy's face. He was alert and obviously enjoying the moment. With Rafe wounded on the ground there seemed nothing else for Dutch to be concerned about. The girl was all his. His lowered the shotgun and reached for Amy with his left arm. When she resisted he slapped across her face and enveloped her with his powerful arms.

'You son of a bitch!' Amy snarled.

Dutch opened his mouth and laughed, showing his yellow teeth. His lips curled back and he grinned like a fanged rattle-snake.

'What will you do now? You have nothing left. Your rescuer lies bleeding on the stones and you don't have a gun. Why resist me?'

Rafe watched with disgust as Dutch forced his lips onto Amy, brutally kissing her. Amy squirmed as Dutch pressed against her, but the outlaw had her locked tightly in his embrace. Rafe noted that Dutch still held the shotgun in his right hand.

The outlaw smacked his lips, savoring the taste of such a beautiful woman. While he kissed her Amy had twisted her right hand up into her vest.

Then Rafe saw that she was indeed a hell of a woman; a woman who left nothing to chance. Amy pulled a pearl-handled derringer from her vest pocket. Her father had taught her well. Pulling back the hammer with her thumb, Amy stuck the derringer up under Dutch's chin.

'I am sick and tired of you pawing at me, you son of a bitch! I am tired of the smell of you and I am tired of looking at your damn ugly face!'

For a moment Dutch looked confused. 'What's this?' he asked.

'My father taught me to always carry a back-up gun,' Amy said.

Dutch cocked an eyebrow, amazement falling across his face like a shadow. Rafe heard the pop of the derringer and Dutch stiffened. When the bullet went up through the underside of his chin Dutch clamped his teeth together. His eyes glazed and blood pooled at the corners of his mouth. He looked like a man who realized he had bitten into poison berries.

He spun in a circle still clinging to Amy. They waltzed toward the precipice for a moment like two unhappy lovers. Amy jerked free and wrestled the shotgun loose.

'This is for Bobby and Ben,' Amy said, her voice shaking with fury. 'Get on your way to hell!'

Dutch sighed, a mournful sigh that turned into a grating noise in his throat that almost sounded like humorless laughter. He leaned toward Amy and put his hand out as if that would stop her.

Amy swung the shotgun up and blew Dutch Williams off the cliff.

★   ★   ★

Black Wolf had disappeared. After an exhausting climb up the rocks Ethan

263

joined Amy and helped her bandage Rafe's wounds. Then Amy bandaged Ethan and made a splint for Adam's broken leg and made a poultice for the wound in his side. An hour was spent looking for Black Wolf but all they found was an indentation in the mossy forest carpet where Ethan had left him. Later Adam said it was an Indian's way to crawl away and die alone, but Ethan never believed it.

They returned to Twisted Oak and Rafe began the long process of healing. Doc Parker cleaned Rafe's wounds and pronounced that he would live. He had cracked ribs and multiple burns, but nothing that would kill him. The bullet wound to his leg would cause a limp, but nothing that was life-threatening, which the doctor said was the best news. Adam and Ethan were also given attention, with Doc Parker commenting that Amy had done a splendid job of bandaging them all up. After being fussed over by the doctor Amy took Rafe to the ranch and made him bunk in the guest room.

The worst part of his ordeal was over and his exhausted body finally took over. He slept for two days. On the third day he awoke to sunlight falling through the window. The sound of a soft footstep had awakened him. Amy came toward him holding a steaming bowl of soup.

'You'll eat all of this soup,' Amy said without looking at him, 'because the sooner you're on your feet the better you'll be.'

'Amy . . . ' Rafe reached for her. She set the soup on the nightstand and took his hand. Now she looked him fully in the eyes, her expression serene and untroubled.

'I don't want to leave,' Rafe said.

'Who said anything about leaving?'

'After I heal, well, I don't think riding on is what I'll do. I found something that means the world to me, Amy. It's you.'

Amy's fingers tightened around his hand. 'You don't have to leave, Rafe.

And if you did I'd follow you and bring you right back!' Now her eyes were moist and she gripped his hand tighter.

'Then I'm staying and I'm proposing,' he said stoically.

Amy laughed. 'I accept. Of course, Pa's going to be mad as a hornet, but I reckon over time you two will get along just fine.'

Epilogue

One afternoon the following September, when the first frost tinted the grass along the riverbank, Ethan propped himself next to an oak and watched his line in the stream in the hopes of catching a speckled trout. He fell asleep watching the sky's reflection drift downstream and very soon he dreamed about the war. He was fighting those old battles again and trying to stay alive when something gently brushed his cheek. He was perplexed and momentarily thought someone had approached him while he was sleeping.

The stream rolled along as always, carrying the reflection of clouds south as the afternoon shadows stretched toward evening. There was a feather on his chest and when he examined it he recognized it as an eagle's feather. He looked around but he was alone.

The next morning he made some purchases in town and set out with Rafe and Amy toward the foothills. A spirited gelding followed the line attached to Ethan's bridle. The day was clear and slightly cool and the sun flashed in the trees like silver and brought the mountains closer. They were silent as they traversed the same trail they'd followed in the spring. After an hour Ethan spotted a rider miles away, high in the rocks, and he squinted through the sunlight but couldn't make out the shape. The rider was visible to them as no more than a speck on the rocks. The rider was gone by the time they rode up a grassy incline. They paused a moment and surveyed the valley they had passed when they had pursued Dutch Williams and his gang.

On the far side of the valley, on a hill overlooking a small lake, were the graves of Bobby Shepard and Ben Wooley. An hour later they reached the graves and Ethan and Rafe secured two small wood crosses to the gravesite.

Amy set Ben's guitar on his grave. For years after, whenever the wind swooped in, some claimed to hear a softly strumming guitar from the high lonesome hills.

Ethan dismounted and untied a parcel from his saddle. He unwrapped the parcel and unfolded a new deerskin coat that had cost him all of his savings. He draped the coat carefully over a boulder. He also left several boxes of rifle cartridges, a new knife, blankets, and two large wool shirts. He untied the gelding and watched as it trotted briefly along an incline before stopping to chew at the grass.

He swept his gaze around the valley once, satisfied that any passing traveler on this trail would find the coat and the other items easily enough. The coat would be useful for anyone living in the high country when the cold winds began to blow. He squinted into the distance, believing for a moment that he saw the figure of an Indian standing on a distant ridgeline. But when he blinked the figure had disappeared. Rafe and Ethan smoked their cigars, each lost in his own thoughts as Amy brushed the tears from her eyes. After a while Rafe and Amy mounted their horses. Ethan was impassive as he squinted into the breathtaking sweep of mountains.

Then Ethan pulled himself into the saddle, nodded once to himself in satisfaction, and together they rode down the trail toward home.

THE END

We do hope that you have enjoyed reading this large print book.

Did you know that all of our titles are available for purchase?

We publish a wide range of high quality large print books including:
Romances, Mysteries, Classics
General Fiction
Non Fiction and Westerns

Special interest titles available in large print are:
The Little Oxford Dictionary
Music Book, Song Book
Hymn Book, Service Book

Also available from us courtesy of Oxford University Press:
Young Readers' Dictionary
(large print edition)
Young Readers' Thesaurus
(large print edition)

For further information or a free brochure, please contact us at:
Ulverscroft Large Print Books Ltd.,
The Green, Bradgate Road, Anstey,
Leicester, LE7 7FU, England.
Tel: (00 44) **0116 236 4325**
Fax: (00 44) **0116 234 0205**

SHOOT, RUN OR DIE!

Jake Douglas

Cody had once fought a cougar to a standstill — bare-handed. He's not a man to mess with. When Curtin and Willis rob him, leave his partner parboiled and burn down the cabin, there is nowhere for the killers to hide. Now a whole town want him for their sheriff — all but Deputy Blake Ross. He makes more trouble for Cody than he's ever seen, enough to plant him on Boot Hill with men he had hunted and killed.